I0533439

Cosmic Shifts

HAIRY & HUNG
COME & YETI

CRYMSYN HART

Purple Sword Publications
Tucson, AZ

All rights reserved. No part of this book may be reproduced in any form or by any electronic means, including information storage and retrieval systems, without permission in writing from the publisher, except by a reviewer who may quote brief passages in review.

This is a work of fiction. Names, places, characters, and events are fictitious in every regard. Any similarities to actual events and persons, living or dead, is purely coincidental. Any trademarks, service marks, product names, or named features are assumed to be the property of their respective owners, and are used only for reference. There is no implied endorsement if any of these terms are used.

COSMIC SHIFTS
Copyright © 2015 CRYMSYN HART
ISBN 978-1-61292-133-4
ISBN 10: 1612921337
Cover Art Designed by Anastasia Rabiyah
Edited by Traci Markou, Shoshana Hurwitz and Jessica Glanville

Published by Purple Sword Publications, LLC
Tucson, Arizona, USA
www.PurpleSword.com

Contents:

Hairy & Hung

Chapter One

The Bigfoot hunters whacked a large stick against one of the trees. The wooden clacks echoed through the forest. Each bang made him wince, and he felt sorry for the poor tree being beaten all because the numbnuts thought they were calling out for the Bigfoot who lived in the area. If they only knew it was pissing him off more than anything else, they might have stopped. But they did not, and he just shook his head. *Stupid hunters haven't figured out that these absurd calls aren't doing anything more than irritating me.* The loud knocks only made his headache worse. Phillip glanced at the sky and saw the sun cresting on the horizon. Splashes of reds and oranges burned the skyline, eating up the twilight blue and the few stars that still dotted the sky. He gripped the tree trunk harder and watched the stars wink out. As the fire of the sun ate up the stars, a silver streak zigzagged across the heavens. At first it resembled a shooting star, and he paid it no mind because he had seen other things like it over the years. As he watched it, Phillip realized that it was not an ordinary falling star or piece of space debris. It was coming closer.

The silvery light emanating from the object was changing colors. It was glowing purple, and its descent was faster than it had been before. He saw a silver ship with amethyst flames licking the metal, turning into blue ones that burned the tops of the trees. The spaceship sailed over his woods, heading for the base of the mountains. If he was seeing this, then so were the hunters. So were other people if they were in the forest. A blast of wind struck him with a strength that nearly bowled him over. Cracking trees and the thundering of the craft hitting the atmosphere made him quake. He felt the disturbance in his bones. The air seemed charged and it electrified the hair on his entire body, making it stand up. The odor of burning ozone stung his nose. The treetops were ablaze where the craft had skipped along the branches. Phillip glanced at the horizon and saw that the night was ending more quickly than he liked. He accelerated his pace to arrive at the crash site while he still had the cover of night.

The crater trail was nearly a mile long. Phillip got to the crash site only to see pieces of metal spread around the valley floor where the vehicle had skidded to a stop. A few rays of sunlight glinted off the metal that was scattered around the hillside. He didn't have a lot of time. All he could hope for was that the hunters would not get to the crash site in the next few minutes, but he already heard the whir of the ATV engines. He picked up his pace, not caring that his footprints were visible in the disturbed earth. The hunters could cast his feet to their hearts' content, and if they found any evidence of him it would still confound them. It helped that the general population did not believe in him.

From the wreckage he knew that this was not a weather balloon, some military aircraft that had crashed, or whatever spin the government put on the happening. If there had been a creature in the alien spaceship, then Phillip did not want it poked and prodded the way he would be if he was ever captured. The hull of the ship had broken into two separate parts. It was not an enormous craft, maybe about the size of two motorhomes put together. One piece was submerged deep within the earth. The other half was spread out over the valley, and he could not see where all the debris had landed. Phillip poked around the buried piece and did not see anything except a few torn pieces of what appeared to be fabric. Wires were hanging out everywhere and sparking. He brushed against some exposed wiring and was shocked. Issuing a grunt, he decided that no one was inside and checked out the other half of the broken craft. There was more of the same: small explosions inside, but no life forms. Phillip sighed, walked around the craft, and saw footprints leading away from the crash site. He knelt down, examining those imprints in the mud, and noticed that they appeared to be canine, almost wolfish. However, instead of four toeprints, there were five. The wolf had an extra toe. No blood dotted the ground that he could see. He hoped that the passenger or the pilot was okay. The roar of engines crept closer. Phillip followed the footprints deeper into the forest, heading up the mountains. The stars were dying, and he would have to find shelter from the elements and the other Bigfoot hunters. The ATVs were drawing nearer and would soon catch up to him.

He quickened his pace and followed the footprints upward. The terrain grew more difficult to maneuver for four wheels, so the humans would have to proceed on foot. Phillip raced up the side of the hill. The canine footprints had stopped and then there were a mixture of wolf and human prints, if such a thing were possible. *Why wouldn't it be possible?* He was possible, so anything was plausible. He willed himself faster, to be one with the wind. One of the best things about his condition was that he had learned to tap into the elements. Phillip could become undetectable in the forest, leave no trace of his footprints or even a shred of hair.

When he crested the knoll, he discovered the perpetrator of the footprints. Sprawled on the ground was the ship's passenger. Phillip neared the prone form and saw a woman with light green skin and long, purple hair. *What in the world? Or not from this world? Where did you come from?* He knelt down and examined her. She was breathing. A dark spot marred her forehead in what he assumed to be a bruise. Her bottom lip was split open, with a plum liquid seeping from it. She was completely naked, with her hair covering her breasts. He pressed his ear to her chest and heard a double thump as though she had two hearts. He glanced at the skyline; the sun was warming his flesh. This was one of the longest times he had maintained his beastly form. Phillip lifted her up gently, held her close to his chest, and followed the mountain ridge higher.

Her body was hotter than a normal human's and nearly scalded his skin. Feeling her heat meant that his hair was receding. Phillip sprinted toward the cave entrance hidden behind a thick layer of boscage and bramble. He pushed through them, feeling the branches scraping along his flesh. He carefully made his way deeper into the cavern until he could no longer see the opening and then slipped through a crack in the wall. Even in his transformed state, he was able to see in the dark. Also, he knew the passageway by heart since he had lived there for so long. They emerged into a circular cavern with a pool in the center of it that led to an underground river. Most importantly, there was an opening in the ceiling that let the light shine down. Shafts of sunlight bounced off the water and also caught the mirrors he had placed strategically throughout the cave so he could have light in the other rooms of the grotto.

Phillip laid the unusual woman down on his bed and made sure she was okay. Her breathing was even, and her double heartbeats thumped strongly. The bruising on her

4

temple had him concerned. How was he going to tell if she had a concussion? He was nothing of a doctor, but knew some herbal remedies. However, he did not know if they would work on the alien female. If the army got a hold of her, they would dissect her the same way they would him. People assumed he was a myth and he made damn sure to keep it that way, but with the encroaching society and modern technology he was slowly losing the battle. One day, he would be discovered.

He studied the woman on his mattress. Her indigo hair had fallen to the side, revealing her darker green nipples. Phillip swept his eyes over the rest of her perfectly lithe body. She had five fingers on her hands like a regular person, had no navel, and besides her hair and eyebrows she was completely hairless. When he got to her feet, he noticed that she had six toes instead of five. Each of them had pointed nails similar to claws. There were no other visible scratches or abrasions on her that he could see. Phillip shook his head and hoped she would regain consciousness. Taking a blanket, he covered her up and brushed his finger along her cheek. Her skin felt soft, like velvet or the soft down of a bird's wing. When he brushed his fingers together, a residue remained that was smooth to the touch. He sniffed them, but came away with no scent.

I can't do anything for her until she wakes up. The best thing for me is to try to get some sleep. He sighed and walked over to the pool. The calm surface reflected his human appearance. Every time he saw his male facade, he was taken aback by it. The face that stared back at him remained the same age he had been when he was a normal man, with brown eyes that had seen too many horrors and light brown hair that curled around his ears. Once upon a time he had known this man, but now he was nothing more than a stranger. The Bigfoot animal was who he had become. Phillip slept mostly during the day because his alter ego was nocturnal, but that didn't mean he was entirely a beast either. Underneath the big feet and the hair, he was still Phillip. Now he was just flesh and bone, flesh that was covered in dirt and muck from a night's hunting for food. He slipped into the pool and washed with a piece of soap he had pilfered from a campsite. Everything he had, he had stolen: piles of books, the clothes and towels he used, even the canned food he indulged in. His home was only one of many he had all over the country where he roamed. This was his main sanctuary because it kept him close to the woman he had loved many centuries ago. Even though she was dust, she lived inside of his heart.

Phillip dunked underneath the water, letting the coolness chill him to the bone. When he was clean, he got out, grabbed a frayed towel, and dried off. His stomach growled, but he didn't feel like eating. He found a pair of bright orange shorts and slipped those on. They brought him little protection, but it was better than nothing. If the woman woke up, he didn't want her to think he was trying to assault her. He figured that when she did wake up she would be disoriented, and hell, he didn't know if they would even speak the same language. She could chirp, for all he knew. Or maybe she was a telepath? If that was the case, what could she garner from his mind?

I can't assume anything until she wakes up. Although I want to be with her, the day is grating on me and I need to get some sleep. He sighed and checked on his guest one last time. When he brushed a stray lock from her face, she stirred, mumbled something, and then lay still. *It appears that she'll be okay.* Glancing around, he noticed his store of bottled water. Phillip grabbed a couple of bottles and placed them before the bed. On a second thought, he laid a shirt and another pair of pants next to the bed so she would see them if she woke up. *At least I can offer her something.* He found an old backpack and laid his head on it. His body was shutting down. He prayed that when he woke she would be okay.

Chapter Two

Alika opened her eyes slowly. Her head pounded, and her entire body hurt from the hard impact. *Stupid sun flares throwing off my instruments. All I wanted to do was get home for Elarna's party. I just* had *to use the short route and cut by Earth because I had to find some stupid gift that she doesn't need. What do you get the woman who has everything in the galaxy?* She tried to shake her head, but it throbbed too much. Alika put her fingers to her temple and did not find a gash. She ran her tongue over her lips and tasted the sour tang of blood from the wound. She barely remembered escaping the ship when it broke apart and hit the ground. All she knew was that her body shifted into its canis form. It was instinct when the situation was dire and she dashed from the crash site, heading to the safety of the mountains until she blacked out.

Sitting up slowly, she waited until the room stopped spiraling and then took in her surroundings. *Great, I'm stuck in some underground cavern with a stinky human sleeping across from me. Gross. What the hell am I going to do to get out of this?* Alika saw that she was covered with a threadbare blanket. Stashes of books were piled around the cave. Weak sunlight filtered in through a gap in the ceiling. Shafts of light bounced off a few strategically placed mirrors to give the room more light. It was a poor showing of technology, but anyone who lived in a cave had some serious issues. Earth dwellers prided themselves on cohabitating in the biggest and most flashy dwellings they could afford. They loaded their lives with material things and didn't care enough about saving their planet. If this one lived in a cavern, then he had to be an outcast in his society.

Maybe it was a good thing that she had woken up in a cave where no one could find her. If located, armies could capture her, steal her technology, and use whatever spare parts they could scavenge from her ship. Of course that would be after they sliced her open, weighed her organs, and garnered whatever medical knowledge they could from her dead tissue. Or maybe it was all a ruse? Maybe they really had brought her to a military facility, and this was their way of keeping her off balance? At the side of her sleeping place was a clear container with some sort of liquid in it and some folded-up fabrics Alika assumed were garments. A shiver rolled down her spine as she contemplated her situation. She wished she had woken up in her canis form. Then she could try to blend in with the indigenous wildlife. The archives on her ship had information about the canine animals on the planet, and her canis form was similar to those on Earth.

"Yark balls," she swore.

Alika rose slowly and surveyed the rest of the cavern. Everything about her felt fine except her head, but she wiggled her toes and flexed her fingers. All seemed to be working. If she had a fully functioning ship, then her health was a quick scan away. It would take seconds. The same with her healing; all she had to do was stand under her medical equipment and the computers would piece her back together. *Stupid, backwoods planet, doesn't even have the right materials or is technologically advanced enough to assist me in fixing my ship, let alone build a new one.* From what she could see, nothing in the cave appeared to be of any help to her.

She did not want to wake the man keeping watch over her. It would be so easy to sneak out and determine whether she was truly being held captive. She was smarter and stronger than the humans. That was a given fact. They were inferior creatures who had barely made any breakthroughs in science that her world had not already discovered centuries before. Her irritation roiled inside of her because it was her fault for taking a shortcut back to Rovan.

She wrapped the thin blanket around her body and walked over to the pool in the center of the grotto. She knelt down and trailed her fingers through the liquid, feeling the cool surface. Alika brought her fingers to her nose, smelling the fluid to make sure it truly was water. There was a slight aroma of sulfur attached to the liquid. She tasted a few drops and grimaced from the tang of the minerals. It was drinkable, but barely so. She guessed that the pool was used by the man for bathing.

A snore erupted from the sleeping male across from her. He did not awaken, but she kept an eye on him. Alika unwound the fabric covering her and dipped her foot into the water. It sent a chill through her, but her body chemistry soon regulated. The bottom of the pool was sandy, and the silt squished between her toes. Small aquatic animals swam around her legs, but she paid them no mind and slipped all the way into the water. Once she was completely in, her internal temperature adjusted so that she became the same temperature as the water. Across from her was a small shelf carved out of the rock with a strange green bar sitting on it. Intrigued, she waded over to it and felt the bottom drop out from underneath her. Her head sank before the surface, and the water slid down her throat.

The coolness touched her head wound, and it helped ease the dizziness that claimed her for a second. Alika came up sputtering and shot a spout of water from her mouth. It landed on the sleeping human. She held her breath. The male opened his eyes. For a moment, she was fascinated by his gaze because she had never seen anyone with brown eyes before. All those on her planet had yellow, black, or orange eyes. Sometimes a genetic anomaly occurred and there was blue or red, but never brown. He continued to stare at her and remained perfectly still. When he started to rise, she retreated to the other side of the pool, pressed against the stone wall. The jagged rocks dug into her back. Her canis self lurked under her skin. Her teeth began to sharpen, but she held back the animal and waited to see what he would do.

The male sat up slowly, obviously trying not to spook her. When he was fully erect, he held up both his hands and smiled at her. She studied him and tried to determine his motives. He said something, but his words were guttural and connected at the same time. It was hard to make out where one word ended and the other began. Alika shook her head, signifying that she did not understand him. Her thoughts raced as she tried to categorize what language he was speaking because there was no universal dialect on this planet the way there was on hers. If only she had been able to recover some instruments from her ship. Maybe she could make him understand that she needed to get back there. Possibly she could salvage some of her equipment and contact her home planet. At least send some communication so that someone could get her off this hick rock and back to Rovan.

The man before her pointed to himself and said a word again. *He's trying to tell me his name. At least that's something I can figure out. What is he saying?* Alika listened harder to hear the sounds he strung together and see how he formed the word.

"Phillip."

Alika forced her lips to form around the strange syllables. The first part was harder for her. "Pil-lup." His forehead creased, but after a moment he nodded and accepted what she had said. She pointed to her chest and said her name. "Alika."

"All-eee-ka." He sounded out the name.

She frowned. It wasn't exactly right, but she wasn't sure a human throat could say her name properly so she was satisfied with the way he said it. "Pillup," she pronounced again.

He nodded and approached the pool. She pulled away even more, pressing against the rock lip. A small growl trembled the back of her throat, and she bared her teeth, wondering what his intentions were. Phillip took a piece of fabric from a space next to him and held it out to her. She remained still. He opened it, covered himself with it, and then placed it at his feet. *He must want me to use that to dry off.* Alika hesitated and then swam over to the other side, clutched the edge of the pool, and studied him. His ears grew red, and he turned around. *Silly humans. I'll never understand them.* She hopped out of the pool and wrapped the cloth around her body. It was pleasantly softer than it looked and absorbed the water from her flesh. When she was done, Alika tapped him on the shoulder. Phillip turned around. She unwound the material and handed it to him. His face became a darker shade of crimson, and he looked away. She sighed. *How are we going to communicate if he won't look at me?* Alika poked him again, harder this time. He glanced at her before racing around and then took the garments that had been folded up and held them out to her, still keeping his eyes down. She was perfectly fine walking around naked, although it seemed that he was not comfortable with it. Then again, he was only wearing something that covered his lower half.

Alika took the clothes, pulled the red top over her head, and stuck her arms through the other two holes. The top stretched across her breasts, but it wasn't uncomfortable. Next, she slipped her legs through the two holes in the blue bottoms and pulled them around her waist. They were a little big, but her hips held them up. When she was done, Phillip smiled and held a cylinder of clear liquid. He twisted the white top off the clear canister, tilted it to his lips, and drank the liquid. He offered her the other container. She took it and mirrored his movements. When the fluid washed over her tongue, she realized that it was water. It had no flavor to it like the minerals she had tasted in the pool did.

After a moment she stopped drinking and gazed at the man before her. She didn't sense any malice from him. It seemed that Phillip was trying to help her, not hurt her or keep her against her will. And yet she still had to make him understand that she had to get back to her ship. Phillip came toward her with a square of material in his hand and reached toward her face. She caught his hand and growled at him again. With his free hand, he gestured toward his head and then pointed at hers. *He's concerned about my well-being. Surely he can't be working for some military organization. He can't be trying to trick me.* Alika released him. Phillip took the cloth and pressed it against her lip. She winced at the sudden pain. He took the cloth away and then added water to it. He said something, but she shook her head and didn't understand.

It was frustrating because he wanted to converse. Alika took the rag and pressed it to her mouth, but her wound was no longer bleeding. She glanced around the cave for something to write with. *I really have to get back to my ship. He brought me here, so he has to know the way to it.* Alika found a sheathed knife. She pulled it out and heard her host make a noise. He had jumped back. She pressed her finger into the point and found that it was moderately sharp. After clearing a space on the dirt floor, she gestured for him to join her.

"Pillup." She drew a crude picture of her ship and waited.

He shook his head and pointed at her drawing. Phillip moved his hands in a motion to indicate that it had exploded. She already knew that. Alika rolled his eyes. *Why can't this go more smoothly?* She pointed at the ship, at him, then at the passageway she assumed led to the surface.

Her host glanced at the ceiling where the sunlight filtered in. The first dappling of stars shone on the horizon, and none of them were the ones she called home. Phillip looked back at her and shook his head, which she understood to mean no. He pointed to the sky and then at himself. Something agitated him that he was trying to tell her from his distressed expression, but she could not figure it out from his hand gestures.

"I'm sorry. I don't know what you're trying to tell me." She threw up her arms.

Phillip took the knife and erased the drawing of her ship. Instead, he drew some humanoid figure that resembled a *gorenaut*, a giant gray ape that lived in the forests on her planet. They were eight feet tall and weighed between six hundred and eight hundred pounds. They were ferocious beasts that even the most seasoned hunters avoided. She had only seen photographs of them, and the environmentalists of Rovan had them proclaimed a protected species.

He gestured at the drawing and then at himself. He took her hands and shook his head once more. This sketch, or whatever he was trying to tell her, had him very disturbed. He spoke again, but it was no use. There was a barrier between them that they could not cross unless she got to her ship and found her galactic translator. She drew the ship again and pointed at it. *Maybe there's another way to get across to him that I have to get back to the crash site.* She touched her throat and then her ear. Phillip studied her. After a moment, he nodded and sighed. Miraculously, he was finally giving in and seeing it her way. *Thank the stars he finally understands.* She smiled, stood up, and walked to the opening that she assumed led up to the surface.

Phillip shook his head. She groaned, agitated that they could not go right away. He peered up at the sky and back at her. Alika gritted her teeth, frustration washing over her. She was so close. He gripped the wall and doubled over as if he was in pain. Alika walked over to him, but when Phillip looked up at her his features had changed. His face had elongated, with a pointier chin and thinner nose. Hair was sprouting all over his body. It seemed that he was growing before her eyes. Alika went to touch him. Phillip grunted and shoved her away from him. *Is he a shape-changer too? From the knowledge I have of this planet, humans don't have that ability.* He pushed away from the wall, and his head nearly brushed the top of the ceiling. While he continued to change, the garments he wore tore and fell away from his hips as they grew wider. Phillip was completely encased in hair and resembled the *gorenaut* more than he did a human male. His nails turned into claws and everything about him was larger, including his feet.

He opened his mouth to say something, but all that came out was an animal call. Phillip touched the side of her face. She saw the intelligence that remained in his eyes. He was not just some animal. She had seen others of her kind lose themselves to the beast within and never make it back. It was a chance they took when they switched their forms. And yet, he seemed to be okay. Phillip moved away and gestured for her to follow.

Chapter Three

Phillip stopped at the mouth of the cave and glanced behind him, hoping the alien woman could keep up. It seemed that the steep incline up to the surface was not bothering her. *Maybe her six toes give her some kind of super grip on the rocks.* The vision of her naked body danced through his mind. He shook his head, trying to push it aside. It had been a long time since he had been with a woman. It did not really matter because he had, and would always be, faithful to the woman he loved. As Phillip thought about his beloved, he tried to call up her image. All he could see clearly was her wonderful smile and the long, dark hair that hung in a braid down her back. He clenched his fists together and tried to recall her more clearly, but the details of her face had paled. Kaylana had slowly been fading from his memory for years, even though he had tried to hold on to her. The love burned in his heart, but it did not account for the loneliness he had suffered. It was nice to have some company in the cave, even though she was a woman from another planet.

Alika. The name flowed through his head like the river winding under the mountains. It was the only word he had understood from what she had said. The rest of it was nonsense. Whatever her language was, it had sounded more like a babbling brook with a few cricket chirps and bird whistles thrown in for good measure. There had been a grunt once in a while too, but he figured that was her frustration coming through. Even his name she was not able to pronounce so well. It seemed that she could not put the sounds together the right way. She had communicated that she needed to go back to her ship. Phillip figured she needed something there. Hopefully, there was a gadget there that could aid in their communications because pointing and drawing things on the dirt floor was not the best way to get his point across.

Alika met him at the cave entrance and smiled. He returned the gesture and knew it was more of a grimace, his lips peeling back from his sharpened teeth. Phillip had frightened many a person with that same look. But they mistook him for some feral animal about to eat them and not for the man under all the hair. His guest said something, but he shook his head and motioned her forward. Phillip took in a whiff of the cool night air. It helped to revive him and keep him focused. He glanced up at the horizon. The stars were in full blaze, beaming their light down to the earth. He wondered if any of them were the one she had fallen from.

His visitor rubbed up against his shoulder and tried to move ahead of him, but he gently grabbed her arm. She spun around and mumbled something, then motioned down the hill. He nodded and put up his hand, hoping she would understand to wait a minute. Phillip touched her chest and then pointed at the sky. Her mouth turned down in a frown, causing little lines to be etched into the corners of her mouth and even deeper ones into her forehead. And yet it made her all the more appealing. *I have to stop letting my mind wander there. I can't be with another woman, and she will eventually return to her home planet. That is, if the authorities don't get her. I'm not going to let that happen anyway.* Their fate would be the same if they were ever caught. Alika stepped away from him and gazed at the sky for a long time. She raised her arm and followed a line of stars. Her finger stopped by the Andromeda constellation and gestured that she meant beyond that. The sadness in her eyes was apparent. She was a very long way from home. Wetness lined her eyes and twisted Phillip's heart even more. Sometimes he forgot he was a man underneath all the hair and big feet, and the animal instincts in him took over. Being with her, Phillip remembered that he was also a man who had feelings. He swiped his finger over her cheek, bringing the tear with it. Alika stared into his eyes, and he was captured by her orange gaze. It seemed like her eyes were on fire. It was a striking feature against her light green skin.

Alika pulled away and motioned back toward the hill. He nodded. Traveling among the brush and dense foliage made it easier for him to blend in so that no one would see him. Phillip moved at his normal gait and did not hear her behind him. He reached the bottom of the hill, glancing back to see if Alika was keeping pace with him. Over the years he had perfected nearly gliding over the countryside and barely leaving an imprint of his large feet. They trekked toward the crash site, and when they finally got closer he heard the hum of engines and generators. Bright lights lit up the area where the ship had skidded and broken apart. The scent of churned earth and ozone clung to the landscape, but the aroma of gasoline and sweat overpowered his senses and made his eyes water. This was one reason he hated to get so close to mankind. They took over the environment and did not care about it. They invaded the land and perverted it, eating up the pristine terrains that provided sanctuary for him and the animals that inhabited the Earth. He growled his dislike of the machinery. The ground rumbled beneath his feet from the heavy equipment being used. Once upon a time, the native peoples had probably seen him exactly the same way that he saw the men who were working on the crash site.

She slipped past him, heading off toward the site. *Great!* He raced after her and ensnared her waist before she could slip out of view. A disgruntled cry escaped her lips, and she struggled to get out of his grip. *Wow, she sure is strong!* Phillip wrapped his other hand around her waist and hauled her back into the shadows so they would not be discovered. She beat her fists against his chest and tried to escape his grasp. He hated that he might hurt her, but she had to calm down.

"Stop," he commanded, but it came out as a grunt.

After a moment, she relaxed and motioned toward the lights. He held up his hands and tried to ease her fears. Phillip knew that she was desperate to get back to her ship. He closed his eyes for a moment, gathering all of the powers that went with his condition. They had developed over time and he had mastered them, to move among the elements and listen to the currents of the Earth. That was how he had learned to become nearly invisible. If he could cloak himself in the wind and move rapidly, then he could get in without anyone noticing him. *Maybe I can take her too. I've never attempted it. First, I have to see what's down there and get back.*

Phillip pointed to himself and then to the illuminated crater. She shook her head and said something. But he put a finger to her lips, and her expression darkened. Alika threw up her hands, turned in a circle, and ran her hands through her hair. Her voice trilled, but she gestured for him to go. Phillip walked toward the treeline, gathering the air around him like a cloak, and drew on the speed that his curse had imparted him. He prayed to whatever god was looking over him and raced into the encampment, trying to keep to the shadows, which was difficult considering all of the lights. Men with guns patrolled the perimeter, keeping watch just in case anyone tried to infiltrate the crash site. Jeeps and ATVs were littered all over the camp. Some kind of building was set up just off to the side, surrounding part of the cracked ship. The sides were heavy-duty plastic. From his observations, he saw men walking around in white smocks, carrying clipboards. They were documenting whatever they had found. A few pieces of metal were scattered about. He wondered if they were something of any value to Alika or just pieces of the hull. In order to get closer, he had to distract the men.

He pressed himself against one of the large pine trees and howled. At first, none of the men moved. Phillip darted to another tree and let out a low grunt. Then he tipped over one of the lights. As it exploded, the men started to scramble. He raced around the perimeter and did the same with the other lights, making the darkness better for his needs. With the light from the stars, he was able to see clearly. When he approached the last one, he saw Alika residing in the shadows. *She must've been watching me while I was putting out the lights. The army is scurrying to figure out what's happening and who is infiltrating the crash site.* All he saw was a blur when she dashed from the darkness. Alika stopped, and he spotted her on the other side of the camp before she disappeared again. Shouting erupted in the clearing, and some of the military men were trying to get the lights back on. Screams and tearing sounds exploded around him. Phillip sped into the middle of the camp and prayed that Alika was all right because he could not see her. Others were dashing around, trying to make sense of the chaos. Gunfire erupted around him. Some of the bullets whizzed past him and narrowly missed his fur.

As he loped through the darkness, one of the men bumped into him. The soldier's eyes widened, and he backpedaled a few steps. The look of shock and fear on his face was almost comical. Phillip smiled and nearly forgot what he was doing there. He glanced down at the crater and noticed some shiny metallic pieces that he scooped up. There was another blur, and something brushed against his leg. Phillip saw an animal that appeared to be a wolf waiting for him just beyond the treeline. Its fur was brown in the moonlight with a hint of green to it. The creature had something in its teeth. He figured it was Alika. More men with guns floundered around. Additional gunshots echoed in the night. The lights were coming back on. It was time for him to vamoose. When Phillip left the encampment, he made sure to leave a couple of foot impressions to confound the scientists. It would make the authorities scratch their heads. Maybe they even got a blurry photo of him that would puzzle them even more. The most important thing was that Alika got whatever she was looking for.

Phillip moved further into the woods where the trees were thicker and no one could see him. When he stopped, he saw the same beast under the light of the sickle moon. This creature was the tallest wolf he had ever seen, and it stood to his hips. Its head was wider than a normal wolf, and its snout held more teeth than any lupine he had ever come across. Its eyes were orange, as if it were a demon hound emerged from the underworld. It had sharp, curved claws, and both legs held six toes. Its two tails were the most beautiful thing he had ever seen on a wolf. There was something in its mouth, and he still carried the few pieces he could find. It glanced at him and then swung its snout toward the direction of the cave. Phillip was all in favor of getting back under cover, where the men could not follow.

He glanced up at the sky. The stars were slowly dimming as they sank lower below the mountains. When they arrived back at the cave, Alika slipped through the underbrush that hid the opening. Phillip had to duck and squeezed in the pathways until he reached the room he called his home. He placed the metallic pieces on his bed and then glanced at the alien creature before him. They stared at one another before she walked over and dropped the things she had in her mouth next to the pieces he had retrieved from her ship. When she stepped back her form twisted, and she was propelled back on two legs. Standing before him, she was almost as tall as his seven foot five frame when in her human guise she barely came up to his stomach when he was a Bigfoot. Her brownish hair receded, and her chest caved in on itself while her green skin reappeared. Her shock of purple hair fell down her back and covered her naked form. Alika's teeth blunted, and her eyes once again captured his attention.

When she was finished with her transformation, he wished that it would be so easy for him to take his human shape. However, that was not to be so. Phillip shivered and tried not to think about the night he had been cursed. He was stuck as an overhairy giant who took human form during the day. He mostly slept those hours away because he had no other reason to be awake. Now he had to be sure that Alika was protected, although by looking at the claws on her feet that had blunted he wondered how much protection she needed. Phillip's passions were rising the more he studied her. He ground his teeth together and focused on something else. His stomach grumbled, and his need for meat grew because the beast in him was letting loose. The longer the night stamped by and he didn't feed, the more it would possess him, and he did not want to lose himself in front of Alika. What would she think of him? *Why do I care what she thinks of me? She's from a different planet and probably has someone waiting for her. Besides, who knows if we're even compatible? I could never be with anyone but Kaylana. My love for her is unending.*

Alika brushed by Phillip, took one of the towels he had, and wrapped it around herself. Seeing her clothed helped him stay centered. She said something that sounded like another bird whistle, a cardinal this time. He shook his head, frustrated that they could not bridge the communication gap. She sat down on the bed again and sifted through the gadgets they had retrieved. Alika brought one of them to eye level, turned it a few times, and pushed a few places on the shard. It resembled nothing more than a twisted spoon, but when she pressed another place it trilled. He jumped. The contraption now faintly glowed purple. She held it up to her ear. Part of it bore into her temple while the rest of it sprouted thin legs the width of a single hair that spread over her ear and down her cheek until it touched the top of her lip. The device sunk into her skin until he could not see it any longer.

Alika spoke a few things directed at him, but Phillip could not understand her still. She sighed, pressed upon her cheek, and a blue glow briefly flared beneath her skin and then faded away. His guest said something again. At first her words were like static. Her eyes scrunched together at the corners, and she waited for him to respond. He shook his head no and then yes. Alika grimaced and uttered a string of words that he assumed from her tone were mixed with frustration and anger. She tapped on the device in her ear. It pushed through her face, walked around in a circle on her cheek, elongated a couple of its tentacles until it shone with a yellow light, and sunk back into her green flesh.

"Can you comprehend me now?" Her voice held a deep, sultry tone that sent shivers along his flesh even under all his hair.

Phillip nodded. Alika jumped from the bed and sprang into his arms, wrapping her feet around his waist and capturing his neck in a strong grip while letting out a squeal.

Chapter Four

A sense of relief washed over her. She collapsed on the platform he called a bed. Luckily, among the wreckage she had been able to find one of the translators; it was a little worse for wear, but at least it worked once she tweaked it. For some reason it had not functioned correctly on the first try. Maybe it was because whatever base language they spoke on Earth was harder for her translator to decipher. At least her host was able to understand her, but Alika was not sure if he would be able to speak in his animal form. On her planet, she could speak mind to mind with others of her kind when they were in their second form. *I don't think his species is as evolved as ours. But maybe.* She stared at his tall body and was amazed at what a massive creature he was. However, she found him to be slightly unattractive because his feet only had five toes, not six. His nails were the same as they were on his hands and not clawed. What kind of beast was he truly? He reminded her of a *gorenaut*, and yet he was vastly different from them. He was certainly tamer than any of the great Goren that roamed her planet in the vast forests and mounts.

"It's a great thing that you can understand me." Alika threaded her fingers through her hair and then down her cheek, checking to make sure her translator remained where it was. It had sunk into her skin; with the minimal damage it had undergone she was not sure it would stay in place, but it seemed to be sticking. The words she uttered in Phillip's language seemed harsh to her ears now that she could hear them. Alika studied the other pieces on the bed. Most of them were useless. A couple could be useful, but if she were going to send a distress call to Rovan she needed more parts to build a communicator. Even then she was not sure if she was going to be able to construct one with the primitive tools on this planet. She had glimpsed some in the building she had nearly toppled that might be of use, although she did not think her host would risk another venture to the ship and she was not about to get captured. Those weapons the other humans had carried could be used in wounding or perhaps even killing her. And she was not about to risk Phillip getting hurt because she was foolish. That meant she would have to go alone. It would be best when he was sleeping. *Yes, that is when I'll go, but when does he sleep? I must learn more about him before I can sneak off. He deserves at least that much.*

The moonlight poured through the opening in the ceiling and illuminated the pool. As it reflected off the water, she saw the beauty of the cave Phillip had brought her to. Small crystals embedded in the walls glittered like the stars she so longed to be among again. Alika sighed. *One day I will get back there.*

Phillip grunted, so she glanced up. He offered her another cylinder of water. Alika accepted it gratefully, twisted the white housing on it, and drank. It was nearly tasteless, but her body needed the liquid. It made her miss the sweet nectar of Baliz wine, pressed from the most wondrous fruit to be found on Rovan. She took another sip of the water and then offered it back to him. He shook his head and gestured for her to keep it.

"Much thanks." Her stomach gurgled, and she realized it had been some time since she had eaten. "Do you have food?"

Phillip cocked his head and then slipped off into another room of the cave. He moved so quickly that she had trouble keeping track of him. It had only been in her canis form that she was truly able to maintain the pace set by her host. When he returned, he held a couple of things in his hands. One was a round orange orb and the other was a gray, shiny cylinder that had some sort of label on it. Alika was not able to read the language printed on the label. He offered her the orange sphere. She took it and sniffed it. The food smelled similar to the Baliz fruit she had longed for. Alika took a large bite and was surprised at the thickness of the skin and the juiciness of the flesh inside of it. The sweetness made her smile. Phillip pushed his nails through the shiny container and pulled back the top, fished something out of it, and slurped it down. She made a face at how he let the contents slide down his throat. He offered the contents to her. Alika forced a smile and then plucked one out delicately, trying not to touch the slimy slices. She wasn't sure what kind of food it was, but it had a sweet aroma, almost too sweet for her palate. She took a tentative bite and found it was appetizing. Alika ate the rest of her slice and then took another. She focused on eating the first object until there was nothing left. Phillip had finished the can and then used the pool to wipe the remnants from his chin.

"Thank you," she said.

He barked something, his lips pulling back over his sharp teeth. Alika figured that he was trying to smile for her. The silence between them was annoying. There was so much she yearned to ask him about, and it just was not possible to communicate. She had had more interaction with others when she was alone in her ship.

"Can you speak at all?"

He gazed at her with those deep brown eyes, and she knew that there was intelligence behind them. Phillip nodded and cleared the dirt floor. He drew a crude figure of himself with the sun next to him, then him being the creature with the moon in the sky. He pointed toward the man image and then his throat.

Alika studied the drawings and realized what he was trying to convey. He was a man by day and the creature before her at night. "So you can only speak when you're a man?"

He nodded.

"Well, you make yourself easily understood." Alika glanced at the pile of metal on the bed and saw the other translator. Maybe it would work. She picked up one of the pieces and broke the end off. She pressed the middle of the circular piece, and a button popped up. When she pushed it, a purple light shot up and illuminated the ceiling. Alika poked the center, and the small circle had four legs. It was the translator's core.

"I might have a solution, but I don't know if it will work. Would you be willing to try?"

His hairy face scrunched up and then relaxed while he thought it over. After a moment, he nodded.

"Could you kneel, please? It will make this easier."

Phillip got onto his knees and looked at her. Alika smoothed the hair where she was going to place the device.

"I'm sorry. This might hurt."

He grunted and looked toward the ground. She placed the gadget in the center of his forehead. The legs pushed into his flesh. Phillip made another sound of pain. His facial muscles twitched. Alika touched the center of the translator, and it wormed its way into his flesh. A howl tore out of his throat. She winced at the sound, but pressed the button again. Its glow softened. Sweat glistened along his top lip where the hair was thin. Soon the device was firmly embedded underneath his skin and not noticeable. Alika ran her hands over his forehead, amazed that the hair was fine, to be sure that the translator was not going to pop out. She trailed her fingers down his cheeks, feeling the strong bone structure underneath. Something about him made her skin tingle, but not in a bad way. She had experienced it on other worlds where their beliefs leaned more toward the mystical than the scientific. It was an odd energy because it was not exactly strong. It seemed to be woven into the very fabric of what he was.

I wonder if I can finally learn more about him.

"I apologize for the pain."

He shook his head. *"There is no pain now. It's just uncomfortable."*

A smile worked her lips up. "Wonderful. It works. I can hear you."

"Hear me? I'm not saying anything."

She laughed. "No, silly." She pointed toward her temple and then touched the translator she had implanted in his forehead. "This allows me to hear your thoughts while you're in this form. I suspect that when you're a man I won't need to read your mind. On my planet, when we're in our bestial forms, we can read one another's thoughts. I thought the translator might help with this."

Alika heard, or rather felt, multiple questions and images pass through her host's mind. They went so quickly that she was not able to make sense of it all. She put her hands to her head and shook it, trying to sort out all of the visions. "Stop. Stop. One inquiry at a time. Your thoughts are moving a little more quickly than what I'm used to."

"Sorry."

"It's okay. We both have a lot of questions for one another. At least this way we can have some sort of discussion. Just take it slow. Fair?"

"Yes." Phillip rose from the ground. He walked over to the other side of the cave and slumped down to the first place she had seen him. Another sense of relief enveloped her because they could finally communicate.

Now she could make her intentions known about obtaining his help and flying off the rock she had landed on.

Of course, there were so many other things she yearned to know too.

"I have much gratitude to you for taking me back to my ship, or what's left of it."

"You're welcome. Did you get all of what you need?" he asked.

"No, I have to go back and gather a few more elements from the wreckage so I can construct a device to send a distress call back to Rovan so they can come and pick me up. There were devices in that building that I could use to help me, but I can't do it alone. Will you help me?"

Phillip rolled his eyes and made a sound of frustration. *"I won't see you get caught by the army. They had guns. They could hurt you. If they catch me, they'll put me on a table and cut me open. I assume they'd do the same to you, considering you're from another planet, and they will want to see what makes you tick. That seems to be the way of all the humans. Is it like that on other planets? On yours?"*

Alika shook her head. "No, we don't automatically dissect other species. We try to learn about them if they visit. We have a defense system in case there is some kind of attack planned, but normally we welcome other visitors. Earth is so primitive. Then again, there's much about this planet that's elementary…" She sighed, searching for the correct term. "That isn't right. How do you say out in the middle of the universe with nothing around it? Where the inhabitants have little intelligence?"

"Boondocks, maybe. So there isn't life on Mars or Saturn?"

She giggled. "Oh no. Well…maybe a long time ago, but everything on Saturn is in ruins. I don't think your people will be able to get there for another two or three centuries. Mars?"

"The red one."

29

"Oh yes. No, nothing lives there either. There were some signs of visitors, but nothing permanent. Right now our people try to avoid Earth."

"Why are you here then?"

She played with a few strands of her hair before she met his gaze. It was nice to know that they could finally talk. As she focused more on Phillip's thoughts, she could easily fall into the wavelengths of his brain. It was comforting to have another being sharing her thoughts. It had been a long time since she had allowed anyone to get so close to her. This was not something she had anticipated; Alika had not had a mate situation for a long time. No one had piqued her interest. How could she tell him that she had been trolling for a birthday gift and ended up being surprised by a solar flare? Would he even understand that? It was obvious that he was smart, but the longer she was linked to his mind, the more she was able to sense the utter loneliness that lived inside of him. Alika was not sure if she had ever met anyone so forlorn.

"I'm here because my ship was blown off course from a solar flare that screwed up my instruments. Before I knew it, I was descending too quickly and wasn't able to skip off your atmosphere back into space."

He scratched his head. It appeared that he picked out something from his fur, examined it carefully, and then ate it. Alika tried to hold back her disgust, but was not able to get very far. Even in her canis form, she did not attract parasites or sample them. *There definitely has to be something wrong with him, or maybe that's just the way he is when he is a beast. Would he be any different as a man? I haven't really observed him. I shouldn't base all of my judgments on just this sole conversation or his hygiene habits.*

"You crashing here made my life interesting. I haven't seen such activity this deep in the woods since one of the hikers got lost and they caught a glimpse of me. News crews

and other hunters came into the forest searching for me. It was rather amusing guiding them around the forest and laying false trails." Phillip hissed and pulled his teeth back from his lips in what she assumed was a laugh because she could hear the delight in his thoughts.

She could not help but smile from his warm demeanor. "Why would you pretend to give others false information about yourself? I would think you wouldn't want to get caught after everything I saw you do today while knocking down the lights. That brings me to now; what are you exactly? I've never come across your species from my database of this planet."

It appeared that his rather large forehead creased. His eyes seemed troubled for a moment. A few images passed through her mind while he was thinking over how to respond to her. He sighed and then met her gaze. *"I've been alone for many years. After a while, I guess I craved some excitement."* Phillip shrugged and grimaced again, but she sensed that he was holding something back. *"There are many names for the beast I've become. Humans call me Bigfoot, Sasquatch, Yeti, Brown Ape, and a few other slang terms they have come up with to describe me. Most people assume I'm a myth. Some believe there are others of my kind."*

"Are there others of your kind?"

Silence erupted between them while he stilled his thoughts. Then she caught a short burst of images. One of them was the picture of a female with long black hair and a bright smile. There were some feelings that he had associated with this woman, but Alika could not latch on to exactly what they meant because the visions were fleeting. *"I don't think there are any others like me exactly. I'm unique. I've never come across them in all my travels, but I have seen signs. It appears that they are a solitary breed. So yes, it is my belief that there are others who resemble what I am."*

"So how do you categorize yourself?"

"Do I need a label? I am exactly as you see me. Beast by night and man by day. Alone for all time."

Alika's heart twisted hearing his words and feeling the deep sorrow of him being alone for so long. She saw the long span of years stream through his mind like neverending space. The vision of him in the cave when a white substance covered the land and him cold and alone, the only solace being the volumes he read and at times a stray animal who would keep him company. Sometimes he was a man and had nothing but his dreams and the memories of the woman he had loved. *This other woman must have been a mate to him. He has not been with another person in so many years.* Although he was a hairy beast standing before her, she saw the man underneath all the hair and wished to bring him a little bit of peace. It was the least she could do to ease to his soul since the poor man had saved her life.

She got up from the bed and crossed the cave to stand before him. He was over seven feet tall, and her head came to the center of his torso. She realized that he could do her real damage. His hand could encompass her head. Those nails could shred skin through to the muscle if they wanted. And yet, Alika knew that he would never hurt her. She placed a hand on his chest, feeling the coarse fur of his pelt. Phillip was remarkably clean, with no insects in his hair or clumps of dirt. She did admire that. *I guess I was wrong about him eating some parasite before.* He jumped at her touch. Alika slid her fingers over the hardness of his abdomen, touching the man underneath.

"What are you doing?" he asked.

She gazed into his deep brown eyes and smiled. "Are you functional?"

Confusion lit his thoughts. *"What do you mean?"*

Alika slid her hand lower over his stomach to his groin, and she felt the semierect shaft and his balls hidden behind a deeper patch of fur. She was happy to discover that his shaft was hairless. She had been mounted by creatures with hairy pricks in the past. It was very uncomfortable with the hair jabbing her in all the wrong places when all she wanted was a pleasant experience. Alika stroked his cock a few times until she felt it firm up. Her smile widened before she looked him in the eye. "You are functional."

A blast of fury seared her mind, and Phillip pulled away from her. *"I am functional, as you say, but you don't have the right to touch me so."*

She shook her head, not understanding why he was fighting her. "You have been alone for so long. Your mate has gone on. Surely you must yearn for companionship. Let me give that to you while I'm here. To show my appreciation for you saving me."

"I won't have you pitying me. Why would you desire me in this form?"

"There is no pity," she said, stripping off the fabric around her and standing before him naked. Alika ran her fingers over her breasts and pinched her nipples until they were pert. From his thoughts, she knew that he was attracted to her. From the reaction of his dick pointing at her, she knew that he desired her. She swayed her hips and banished the distance between them, pressing her body against his. His thick pelt scratched her in a good way and made her warm in the chilly cave. She slid her hand over his length again, took one of his hands, and placed it on her breast. "I find you pleasing in both forms. I enjoy big, strong men. So do many women on my planet. Goddess Dirvan knows that there aren't enough to go around. You would do quite well there, have many women waiting to pleasure you. We are a population where only one male child is born in ten thousand. Come now, Phillip. Let me do this for you." She stood up on tiptoe and pushed her lips into his.

He did not respond, but his cock hardened and hit the middle of her chest. Now that it was fully engorged, she could see that it was twelve inches long and three inches around. Good. She enjoyed well-endowed males. Alika rubbed herself against him and bit his bottom lip. Her canis side was emerging. Her teeth shifted a little bit, getting pointier. Her nails grew into claws that she dug into Phillip's back. It was then that he thrust his tongue into her mouth and returned her kiss with a fierceness that rivaled any of her past lovers. There was a hunger in him that was entwined with the beast that lived within him that wanted to fuck and nothing else. But she sensed that the man was there too, fighting to keep a leash on the animal. He wrapped his claws around her back and raked them down her flesh. She grunted at the pain and welcomed it. He broke the kiss, panting slightly, and glanced at her.

"Are you hurt?"

She shook her head. "No. It feels good. Don't stop now."

Alika grabbed his head and brought his lips back to hers. She plunged her tongue into his mouth and wrapped it around his long, curved fangs. Phillip slid his fingers down her back and grabbed the mounds of her ass. He squeezed them and lifted her up against the cave wall without breaking the kiss. The coolness of the cave wall helped her to focus. He nibbled at her lips with his teeth, trying not to draw blood. Phillip was trying to be gentle, but he was losing control. The hardness of his cock pressed into her belly. She tangled her fingers in his fur and stroked his prick at the same time. He threw his head back and cried out. His howl filled the cave. She grinned and knew that he was close to coming. Alika guided his dick inside of her pussy, taking what she could of him. Phillip locked gazes with her and then thrust into her.

A little more of her canis self slipped out, merging with her alien self. Her legs grew longer, and hair pushed through her flesh. He did not seem to see or care about that. Now that she was a little taller and longer in length, she found that she could accommodate his entire shaft. The man reflected in his eyes had disappeared. His thoughts were all bestial. She didn't care. Her rational side escaped her as the animal within her came to the front. She threw back her head and clasped her feet around Phillip's waist, rubbing her toes over his furry ass. He licked the line of her throat, biting here and there, until he broke the skin on her shoulder. At that moment, he drove into her all the way.

Alika cried out as her big-footed lover hit her pleasure centers. She swiveled her hips and right when he plunged into her for the last time, she felt the warmth of her release also shoot through her. Alika squeezed her eyes shut when his claws pierced her flesh. He bit down into her shoulder once more, sending another jolt of ecstasy into her. A deep yowl came from his chest. She followed a moment later, feeling her muscles clench around his shaft. Alika rocked her hips against him one last time. White-hot heat rode her spine and rocked her body. It took her a few minutes to return to herself. When she did, she found that she was lying on the bed. Her savior was across the room using the wall to hold himself up. He was breathing hard.

"Are you all right?"

"I should be asking you that. I got carried away."

"I'm fine."

He grunted. *"Good. Stay here and use the pool if you wish. I must hunt."*

"Let me go with you."

"No. I know the terrain, and there are hunters looking for you. Rest. I will be back."

Alika nodded and knew that he was correct. There were people searching for her. Phillip exited the cave, leaving her to think about what had happened between them. It had been wonderful and a good release. Now she had to focus on the task at hand. How was she going to send a distress call with the meager technology that she possessed?

Chapter Five

Phillip glanced up at the sky and saw that dawn was not far off. The sounds of helicopters filled the lightening sky, and the tang of fresh blood lingered in his mouth. He carried two rabbits he had caught to bring back to Alika. Now that he had fed, he could think coherently. It also helped that it was near dawn. His human rationale had returned, and it was easier for him to think clearly. It was tough to believe that he had coupled with her, but it seemed that she had enjoyed it. Something about her cut through his animal urges, and she was able to connect with him the way no other had. When he thought of Kaylana, he could not recall her face. He shook his head and wondered if she would care if he was with someone else.

Not that it matters, because Alika is going home eventually. She will do whatever it takes to get off this planet. The way she talks about Earth as if it was a swampland, I know she's unhappy. He studied the search pattern of the helicopter and noticed that it was getting closer and closer to the cave. The army was looking for them. Phillip would have to be careful and make sure that he was not discovered. He clutched the rabbits and gathered the power that came with his curse. Before the sun fully broke over the horizon, he sped along the backside of the mountain and concentrated on being one with the air so even the instruments of modern men would not be able to track him. Sometimes he wondered if there was any kind of explanation to the magic he carried within him. Maybe one day technology would catch up to him, and they would discover what he truly was. Or maybe they could make it so that the curse was broken, and he would be a man again. Alika had mentioned that on her world her people had two forms, and he might be appreciated there. *Funny to think of a world where there are more women than men. I wonder what they do.*

The air wrapped around him and cooled his skin, even through all the hair. Phillip moved with an ease that came with years of practice and glided among the trees, staying out of range of the helicopters. Phillip entered an obscure entrance to the cave system and slipped through the brush, making sure no trace of him was left behind to track. Traversing the caverns, he felt the sun rising and was transforming back into a man. When he walked into the cave, Alika was sprawled on the bed with a sheet loosely wrapped around her; it clung to her thigh and left most of her back exposed. He saw where he had clawed her, but the marks did not seem to be too severe. Rays of light caressed her jade-green skin. His throat tightened at how beautiful she was. She might have been from another world but they fit together so well, and she had not balked at his claws or his size. It had felt wonderful to be inside of her. He had become lost to all his base desires and let the beast take over completely. Phillip set the rabbits down by the cave wall and slipped into the pool, hoping not to wake her. He dunked his head under the water. When he came up, he felt along his forehead where she had placed her communication device. Phillip did not feel any protrusions where the device was. It was nice to be able to speak with her, even if it was with his thoughts. He knew that she had picked up on some other things by their connection. Phillip yearned to ask her more, but did not want to disturb her.

After he bathed, he skinned the rabbits and brought them to another part of the cave to drain. He stole what food and water he could from campers he ran into and scared away. At times he ventured into the nearest town and bought supplies, but those were few and far between because he could not be caught out after sunset. Most of the time if he was not too lost to the beast, then he would remember to catch something and bring it back to his lair. He would rather that the meat be cooked, but the beast wanted it bloody. He had taken down a stag earlier that night, ate what he could, and left the remains for the wolves to scavenge. He was no longer hungry, but he was not sure whether Alika was hungry or if she wanted the game raw or prepared. At the moment, he could not take the chance of building a fire because the helicopters would see the smoke.

Instead, he wrapped a towel around his waist and sat across from Alika, grabbed a leather-bound journal, and wrote about his experiences with the mystery woman that had crash-landed in his backyard.

He must have fallen asleep because he awoke a few hours later, and Alika was not on the bed. A jolt of panic rushed through him. Phillip bolted into the other room of the cavern, but did not see her there either. He inhaled and caught her scent leading from the cave toward the surface. He followed it to the entrance, and his worst fears encompassed him. She had gone to scout out the area and would be caught. He raced back into the cave and found some clothes, slipping into some jeans, a T-shirt, and an old pair of hiking boots he had stolen from a camper years before. Phillip ascended to the surface and scoured the ground for any trace of Alika, finding her footprints lightly pressed into the dirt. Years of practice had made him a good tracker. He followed the indentations up the mountain and away from her crash site, but toward a familiar path he had not traveled in a long time.

His pace quickened. The earth lent its strength and kept him grounded. The higher he climbed, the cleaner the air became. He prayed that the helicopters were not circling, and that they did not happen to notice a green woman walking around during the day. When he finally came to the precipice, it opened up onto a flat verdant surface with several old pines shading the spot almost in a circle. Phillip stopped when he discovered Alika bowing before a pile of stones. The alien woman was clothed in an oversized T-shirt that covered most of her arms and a furry yellow winter hat with ear flaps that was low over her face. A pair of large purple sunglasses covered most of her face, and a pair of jeans that seemed to be too small for her hugged every curve. If a hiker or the authorities had come upon her, they might not have noticed that she was different. He prayed that that was the case.

After watching her press her palms over her eyes and then splay her fingers upon the dirt several times, he coughed to capture her attention. Alika stopped and when she spotted him, a wide smile spread across her lips. It lifted his heart. For the first time in a long time, he wanted to be with someone again. To not be so alone was something he had marveled at for a long time. He had wrestled with his heart and wondered if it were ever possible to love once more. Who would ever want a monster? Maybe with Alika his curse could be broken. Then again, maybe it was worsening because she would leave him alone eventually. It was not a good thing to open his heart to her. Phillip pushed the thoughts of her staying and maybe making a life with him away because it was not going to happen. If she did stay, it would be a constant battle trying to hide her presence so that she would not be caught. The best choice for her was to find a way off the planet and return home.

"What are you doing here?" asked Alika.

"I should be asking you the same thing." Phillip crossed his arms over his chest. The irritation he felt was rising like hot bile up his throat. He tried to stay the fury, but it blazed through him. A breeze came up, and on it he heard the echo of the machines near the ship. "You shouldn't be out in the open. Someone may see you. They're watching the mountains. I can hear them using their machines, and soon they'll identify your blood that was left behind or maybe follow your footprints if they haven't already."

Her brow furrowed. "Pillup, it will be okay."

"Alika, you don't know that. And you're not saying my name right. I couldn't tell you before. It's not Pillup."

"Oh, sorry. How do you say your nomen?"

"Phillip."

She pursed her mouth around his name. "Pillup."

He shook his head, feeling his frustration ebb. He knelt by her and reached for her, but stopped. "Can I?"

"You may touch me."

He cupped her face between his hands and felt the smooth skin. Their encounter, even with him being a beast, enthralled him. His heart twisted at the rise of feeling that swept through him. A small moan slipped from his lips at the joy that he was now able to touch her satin cheek and inhale the citrus perfume that he associated with her. Alika's orange eyes sparkled in the daylight. He brushed his thumb over her bottom lip. She inhaled and waited. Phillip used his thumb and forefinger to pucker her lips. Alika was very patient with him while he manipulated her mouth.

"It's Phillip." He pursed his lips and exaggerated the *ph* sound so that she could get an idea of the reverberation she was having trouble with.

"Ph…illip." She pronounced slowly but got the sound right. Her accent was more noticeable, and she swallowed some of her sounds. He doubted that he could do as well with her native tongue.

Phillip watched her mouth form around his name. When the sound came from her lips, a spear of desire shot right to his cock. He could not help but capture those lips in a rough kiss. Alika seemed surprised, but she did not shy away from him. Instead, she slipped her fingers along his head and then balled her hands in her hair. She pulled him down on top of her. He was afraid that he would crush her because she was so small compared to him, even when he was human. Alika plunged her tongue into his mouth until they touched and tasted one another. His prick firmed up at the thought of entering her once more, this time while he was human. When he saw the makeshift headstone he had erected for his beloved, all the passion drained from him. Guilt sufficed his being knowing that he had desecrated Kaylana's grave. Phillip sat up and shuffled off of Alika. The spell had been broken. He and Kaylana had been happy together until her father had declared him the devil against the tribe. His beloved had sacrificed herself for him, and he had nearly lost his mind.

Phillip held his face in his hands and could not stop the tears. Kaylana's beautiful smile warmed him. What would it have been like to be in the afterlife with the woman he loved? All because of him, she was dead. If only he had never come into her life. Those were questions he had asked himself for a long time. Four centuries of nights had passed, and he was alone.

A soft hand caressed his cheek. He glanced up and saw Alika peering at him with concern and curiosity in her eyes. "Why do you cry? Is it for the one who lies underneath these stones? The one you care about?"

"How do you know about her?" he asked.

She ran her fingers along his temple. "I saw her in your mind. Your thoughts are open to me more so when you're in your second form. Now it's much more guarded. I saw your mate and felt how you cared for her. This is where you brought her because this was her favorite place to look out over the land."

He nodded. "Yes. There used to be blue flowers that grew here along with wild blackberries. She loved them. We would climb up here and eat them until the juice stained our faces. Her father didn't approve of me. He saw me as one who wanted to rip his world apart because I was a soldier. It was my fault she died, trying to save me from her father. When she died I went insane, killed a few of the tribe, and then he cursed me. Sometimes I come here to think and be close to her."

"That's why you chose these caves, because you wished to be close to her?"

"Yeah."

"But she has gone beyond. Why do you hang on to the past?"

"Don't you have feelings? Haven't you ever loved anyone? Do you know the emotion?" The anger rising in him was tricky to keep out of his voice. With all the questions she asked, he wondered if she even had a heart.

Alika placed a finger on his lips and drew one of his hands to her chest. "I have two hearts. L-lov-ve," she tripped over the word, "we call it *trima*, but from what I've garnered from your thoughts and feelings it is the same thing. This emotion makes you see stars and fills your world so that you see nothing else. I had a mate, a very long time ago, and he lost himself to the canis...the beast inside of my people. I share your loss and came here to show my respect toward the one who you lost and to the mate I will never see again. You remind me of him in some ways. You feel my hearts beat, Phillip, and know that we are not so different."

She brushed her lips over his. They were sweet, and it lifted his dark mood. He had not expected to hear that she once had a man who loved her, so she understood his heartache. Alika pulled away and left him wanting to feel her sweet mouth on his again.

"Thank you."

"For what?"

"For understanding. For showing me that Kaylana isn't here any longer, and that I've been holding on to her for a long time."

"You can let her go. She will always be in your heart, as he is in mine."

Phillip smiled and felt that some weight had been lifted off his shoulders. Alika sat back on her heels and gazed at him. "You took a chance coming here." He glanced down and realized that from there they could see her vessel.

She shrugged. "I was careful. Your military is too busy trying to collect the remains of my ship."

"You're going to leave, aren't you?"

"I do not belong here. I must get the technology I need to send a distress call. Can you help me with this?"

He sighed and glanced at the sun. There was time for him to go into town if he had transportation and the money to get her the things she desired. However, the easier way was to collect what he needed from the military. That opened up a whole other load of trouble, but it was the only way she was ever going to get the equipment. "I can try, but it'll be difficult to infiltrate the camp. But I have an idea. You'd have to stay behind." Phillip got up and dusted his jeans off. He went another way until he was higher up and then observed the crash site.

The activity was not so swarming today. It seemed that it was fairly deserted. He prayed that he could get in and out. He glanced at the sky again and would have to act quickly. Phillip worked his way back into the cave. In one of the stashes he had collected over the years, he had something he hoped would be the thing. A few years ago, he had come upon an injured man who had been wearing the clothes of an army man. There had been a fire, and the National Guard had been called in to assist. He had helped the man and then taken his clothes. Phillip had gotten the blood out and kept the uniform. He stripped off his clothes and pulled out the uniform. It was just about his size, down to the boots. When he was done, he noticed Alika standing there.

"Wow. That uniform does something for you."

"Will you stay here while I go?" He chuckled.

She nodded. "Yes, but you need to get me a computer, some tools, and anything else you can carry."

"All right! I'll be back."

When he came to the perimeter of the crash site, he saw more doctors than he did military people. He slipped closer to the plastic wall of the makeshift buildings the army had erected. His boot hit something metal. He picked it up and shoved it into his pocket. A man with a rifle strode by him and nodded. Phillip nodded back and kept on walking. He strolled by one of the openings and glanced around to see if anyone was watching. They were not, so he crept inside one of the tents. It was empty. Several closed laptops lay on the table. He spied a bag, grabbed it, and slipped one of the computers into it. Phillip heard voices coming toward the tent and moved outside quickly through another entrance. A white-coated doctor with wire-rimmed glasses and a receding hairline noticed Phillip.

"Can I help you, soldier?" the doctor asked.

"Just checking to make sure everything was secure."

The balding man stared at him. Phillip saw the questions in his eyes, but he did not waver and kept perfectly still. "Okay. Has the captain given you stricter orders to watch out for tall hairy creatures?"

Phillip cracked a smile. "Always have to keep a lookout for anything suspicious. Have you seen anything unusual fall from the sky again?"

The doctor laughed and patted him on the shoulder. "Good man. Tell your captain to come have a drink with me later. I have some findings we need to discuss."

Phillip hugged the bag closer to his body and glanced around to see if there were eyes on him. Voices filled the tents behind him. He peered up at the sun and prayed that he would have enough time to get back to the cave. At the edge of the encampment, he went into another tent. A cell phone and some instruments were laid out on the table. Other medical instruments and things he had not seen earlier surrounded the gadgets he figured were also from Alika's ship. He gathered those up quickly and put them into the bag along with the cell phone. He prayed that that would be enough for Alika. He had spent too much time in the company of men and they were making him uncomfortable, even though years before he had traveled from England and had been a captain in the Queen's army. That was another life. What it was like to be completely human had somehow escaped him. In the early years, he had searched for a way out of his curse. He had scoured the world, traveling as a man and as a beast, but no matter who he had spoken to, wise man, guru, or psychic, they did not know how to break his curse. When he had tried to speak to other Native American shamans, they would not even see him. It seemed that they knew what he was and cursed him even more. It only made him lonelier.

"Solider, what are you doing away from your post?"

He froze and searched for a reason to give the commanding officer behind him. He turned slowly and tried to look official. The man before him was clearly the one in charge. "Sir, one of the doctors asked me to bring them some equipment."

"Why haven't I seen you before, Private?"

Oh shit! "I just came in this morning, Sir."

The captain stared at him. Phillip stiffened. The captain knew that something was wrong. Phillip could feel it in his bones. The other man studied him, and Phillip tried to stay in character. His heart slammed into his chest, and his throat went dry. All he could do was pray that he would not be discovered. The officer was about to say something when an alarm went off that blared through the camp. A blur went by his left side. Another army man ran toward the captain and stopped before him to salute and then catch his breath.

"Sir, something's been sighted along the perimeter of the camp."

"Did you see another fox again, O'Brian?"

O'Brian's eye twitched. He was terrified of the captain. The other man flicked his gaze to the side, and Phillip saw a series of flashbulbs going off around the edges of the camp. Where the large lights had been the other day, they had been replaced with the motion-activated kind. He saw more flashes and a glimpse of two tails. Alika was creating a diversion for him. The camp around him was scrambling. The captain stared at O'Brian.

"No, Sir. We think it's the creature."

The captain glanced between both of them. Phillip saw the hesitation on the captain's face. "Well, what are you waiting for? Go catch it. This is what we've been waiting for. Go catch the beast."

O'Brian did not wait, and neither did Phillip. He dashed off in the same direction. Men swarmed to the perimeter of the camp. He hugged the bag closer and headed back into the forest. When he was clear, he stopped at the nearest tree and caught his breath. Gunfire erupted around the crash site. There were shouts. Alika ran toward him in the form of a large wolf. There were men following her on ATVs and gaining on her.

He had to help her.

Phillip jumped and heaved the bag into the tree so he could get it later. They were racing right by him. Alika dashed past him and then he jumped out in front of the ATVs. They swerved to avoid hitting him. One of them broke to the left and ran straight into a large boulder. The other ATV shot around him, still heading toward Alika. Behind them were men on foot trying to keep up with the ones on the ATVs. Phillip bolted after the one lone man left on the ATV. He came to the side of the mountain and found the abandoned vehicle where the rocks were too jagged for the wheels. A gunshot sounded in the distance. Phillip raced toward the sound. He crested the rock and saw Alika lying motionless on the ground, slowly turning back from her animal form to her human one. The army man was speaking into his radio.

"Yes. I've got it. And you won't believe what it is." The man went over to Alika and poked her with his rifle. "Whatever you are, you are one sexy alien."

Hearing that angered Phillip. He skidded down the embankment and leaped on the man. It was all about saving Alika from the likes of the man trying to hurt her. A green liquid seeped from the wound. Phillip knelt down and scooped Alika into his arms. He hugged her close and glanced at the man he had felled. He felt a little guilty, but when he saw the rise and fall of his chest Phillip assumed he would be okay. Now his first priority was the limp woman in his arms. Her naked form was enticing, but he heard shouts behind him. The army was not going to stop until they had her. He scrambled up the mountain until he came to a little-known path. It wound around the backside of the mountain and then took them out of sight. The army was never going to give up. It was settled. There was no way for him to secretly hope for her to stay and for them to make a life together. The military had pictures of her and probably of him too, but he could take care of himself.

He wound down the path, hidden by a thicket of trees. The sun was going to be setting. Phillip had until then to tend to her wounds. She was breathing evenly, which was a good sign, but the wound on her shoulder was still seeping green blood. He came to a small opening in the cave system and slipped inside, holding her close. Darkness enveloped him. He worked his way back to the place he called home for now and rested her on the bed. Phillip grabbed an old towel and soaked it in the pool of water to clear away the blood. A bullet had grazed her shoulder. He glanced around and saw an old first-aid kit he had stolen from a hiker many years ago. The case was rusted, but the essentials were still good. Inside was a bandage and some antibiotic ointment, but he was not sure what the expiration date on it was or whether it would react with her physiology. When he thought the bleeding had stopped, he covered her with a sheet. Then he felt around her head and came away with a large bump. Hopefully, she did not have a concussion and would be able to wake up without any medical attention. The knowledge he did have was rusty, and it came from old books. The time he had to wander the earth and exist as a Bigfoot had given him time to read and see many things he would not have been able to do when he was human. However, all of that knowledge and experience could not help him save an extraterrestrial woman who had made him see that there was more to life than being an animal.

While Phillip scoured his cave, a dark thought slid over him. There had been a lot of blood from her head laceration. The military could follow that and find them both. He could not let that happen. That meant that he had to bring them deeper into the mountains. Only one other cave was safe. It was a long journey even by himself. Although it would bring them miles from the crash site, it would also throw off the scent. He hoped. Phillip quickly gathered some clothes, provisions, and the first-aid kit into one of the large knapsacks. He also grabbed a sleeping bag. Hopefully, it would be enough. He slung the backpack and the sleeping bag over his shoulders and then glanced at Alika. There had to be some way of holding her close to him and leaving his arms free. Something in case they were following him and he needed to hide. Phillip grabbed a couple of lanterns. They would need them if they were traveling deep in the caves.

He then took a sheet and wrapped it around himself, tying it at his shoulder to make a large sling. He lifted Alika into it and positioned it so that she was hugging him. Instinct told him that he did not have a lot of time. Phillip prayed that the army did not have any experienced cavers among them, albeit it would take them a while to catch up with him and learn the way through the caving system. There were nooks and crannies in the mountains that even the most experienced cavers did not know about. He could go back and get the computer and the other things he had stolen from the army camp. His senses told him that they were amassing already to come and find him. It would only be a matter of time. He walked toward the back passageway and then glanced at the cave he had called one of his homes for a long time. It might not have been the most comfortable one, but it was the closest one to his Kaylana. Saying goodbye to it, he was saying goodbye to the woman he had loved for so long.

Chapter Six

Alika slowly opened her eyes. She was aware of the world moving and swaying in the darkness and was nestled up to a very hairy male. As she inhaled, Alika realized that it was Phillip. The last thing she remembered was being chased by men with guns, trying to distract them so that he could escape. He had told her to stay put, but after he took so long she had a bad feeling so she went down to see if there was anything she could do. However, she had not assumed that they would be ready for her. The military had almost caught her on the vehicles they had used to chase her. Phillip must have distracted them because when she glanced behind her only one of them was following her. On foot she had lured the other one away, but he had wounded her. The pain had been a shock. She had lost her footing and hit her head. After that, she did not remember anything. When she looked up and saw nothing but darkness, she guessed that they were underground and that Phillip was carrying her. When she moved, pain shot from her shoulder all the way down her arm. *I have to be hurt worse than I realize.*

Squinting, Alika tried to see where she was going. Her eyes adjusted so she could only make out darker shades of black. She placed a hand on Phillip's shoulder, and he stopped.

"Where are we going?" she asked.

He grunted. *"You've been unconscious for several hours. We're heading to another cave where I hope they won't find us."*

Alika nodded. It was a good decision for them to move. "I'm sorry I brought these problems down on your shoulders."

"It's not a problem. Men are meddlesome. This isn't the first time I've been hunted, and it won't be the last. How are you feeling?"

"Okay. You can put me down now." She ran her fingers through his pelt and over his snout. He pulled his lips back into a snarl, but she figured it was a smile. It was also apparent that he was getting aroused from his large member poking her side.

Phillip set her down gently. *"Stay close to me. We're at a perilous part of the journey. It won't be much longer now."*

"Do you have any light?"

He bellowed and then fumbled for something. After a second the sudden illumination hurt her eyes, but it allowed her to see. They were in a very tight space that her savior had to stoop in. When she looked down, they were on a very thin ledge that wound around the crag they were on. The path was about to open up in a few steps. Phillip carried a couple of items. Maybe some of them were the things he had obtained from her ship. He handed the light to her so she could examine her wounds. They were dressed. Alika felt the bump on the back of her head and the dried blood that matted her hair. The tight quarters and being so far underground were stifling. She could only imagine what Phillip was feeling in his second form.

"Thank you. Lead the way."

He nodded and then squeezed through the narrow space. Alika was surprised that he was able to because it was challenging to press between the constricted passageway. They finally came to where the ledge turned into an open expanse. She swung her light around, and the darkness swallowed the illumination. The grotto seemed to go on forever. If she listened, she could hear the sound of running water. It had to be an underground river. That must have been where the pool had come from. If she had her instruments, she could easily pull up a topographical map of the area. Still, she followed behind Phillip until they came to a stop.

"What is it?"

"The rocks have shifted since my last excursion into the caves. I have to move the boulder, or we'll have to go back."

Alika glanced at the rock. It must have weighed a couple of tons. "Are you going to be able to move it?"

He shrugged. *"I don't know."*

She stood back and waited. He got a grip on the rock and tried to pull it out. His muscles strained and bunched under his fur, but the boulder was not moving. She angled the light to the top of the rock and noticed a few smaller stones above it. After he grunted and groaned nothing was happening, so Alika poked him.

"Try moving those small ones."

Phillip reached up and plucked out a few of the lesser rocks. Dirt rained down around them, and grime settled on her skin. The big one shifted down some, creating an opening wide enough for her to squash through. It was too tiny for Phillip, even in human form. They did not have the time to wait for the sun to rise. *Now would be the time for me to have stuff from my ship. Then maybe I could blast it.* "Did you happen to get anything from my ship while you were in the camp?"

He nodded and dug into the backpack he carried with him. He handed her the pants he had on before he turned into his animal self. She patted down the fabric and found the pockets. Alika pulled out metal bits that were nothing more than pieces from the outer hull of her ship. Those were no good. There were two minute purple bits that clung to one of the metal pieces. She pulled one off and was glad that they were still dry. Explosive tamerite was one of the birthday gifts she had on board for Elarna. It was stable when it was dry, but when it was exposed to moisture it was volatile. She placed one of the dots on the large rock.

"What will that do?"

"It's one of the reasons my ship is in pieces. Some coolant must have gotten on it when I hit the atmosphere. When I landed…well, I'm surprised I was in one piece."

"Won't that cause another cave-in if it is so strong?"

Alika sighed and scraped off a little bit more, thinking about the size of the rock. "I think this should be okay. You need to get back. It'll only be a few seconds before it detonates." She gathered the spit into her mouth, backed away a few steps, then spat onto the explosive. Her aim was off, and she missed.

Phillip chortled behind her.

"I like this game. Move away; I have better aim than you do."

He stood and used his hand to usher her behind him. He was being a hero and trying to be chivalrous to protect her. Alika peered out from behind him while he spit at the rock. It hit right on the tamerite. The faint sizzle of the explosive being activated echoed in the cavern.

She jerked on his arm and pulled him back. They had fifteen or twenty seconds before it was going to go off. They rushed backward and hid in a small nook while he was shielding her. Alika covered her ears. The whole entire cave shook. Bits of dirt fell into her hair, and rocks pelted her. The earth beneath her shivered and she waited for it to fall away, but it didn't. Phillip moved out of the way. The rock was just smaller pebbles, so they could pass through the corridor. She gathered up Phillip's bag, and they moved forward.

"That made quite a bang. I wonder if they detected it. I'm sure someone felt the earth shake. It would be noticeable with all the equipment they have at the campsite."

Alika agreed with him. It had been a large risk by blowing up the boulder, but it had been the only way to go onward. They came to a narrow outlet that Phillip slipped into. She would have missed it if she was not following him. She went after him slowly and felt her way around the rocks. They were wet. Water was moving swiftly near them.

The air grew light while they ascended. When they finally emerged, she saw the night filtering through small holes in the cave ceiling. There was a waterfall at the edge of the cave. Some plants grew along the side of the walls. This was a lush spot that she could see them staying in. Phillip did not stop. Her guide steered her further into the mountain. They wound around a path that led behind the waterfall. She hefted the bag over her shoulder, and they still tramped upward. After what seemed to be hours, they stopped. She shone her light into a hole.

"We must climb through there. About twenty feet, and then there is a ledge you drop onto. Wait for me there."

He lifted her up and she shimmied through the hole, crawling on her belly. The passageway was large enough for Phillip to get through. She came to the end of the duct and found the sill she landed on. After a moment, she heard Phillip coming through. When he came down onto the shelf, he jumped from there to the cave floor.

"Jump. I shall catch you."

Alika shined the light down to the floor and saw that it was quite a drop. She stared at the creature before her, more animal than human on the outside, but his heart was pure. She did not hesitate and leaped into his strong arms. His fur pressed against her flesh and made her itch, along with the dirt she had on her from the explosion. All she craved was for some water to bathe in. It would make her feel so much better. Phillip set her down and took the light. He led the way around a corner and stopped a little way down. The cave

55

they came to was even more beautiful than the last. Several holes in the cave ceiling let the light in so she could see the crystals embedded in the wall. Large quartz grew along the cave walls. Their power blasted against her flesh. Crystals held energy. Her people had harnessed it ages ago. This whole cave was a conductor. If she had the right equipment, she could use the energy in the crystals to boost her signal. First she had to be sure that she had the right equipment to get it all done.

"We'll stop here."

Alika trailed her fingers along one of the crystals and felt it vibrate under her touch. Such raw and untapped power was an amazing find. With the right equipment, there was hope that her distress call would get someone's attention. Now all she needed was the machinery. Phillip set the bags down, laid out a layer of silky fabric, and then dug into his bag. He pulled out containers of water, food, and some clothes, which he handed to her. She had no qualms about being without garments, but it bothered him so she slipped on the shirt and shorts so she was no longer naked. From there, he leaned against the wall and motioned for her to sit down.

She took one of the containers of water, broke the white strand around the lip, and twisted the cap off. She took a sip and then offered it to Phillip.

"No. You need it. I can get more."

"This place, are you sure no one will be able to find it?" Alika asked.

"It has not been disturbed by any humans since I've been coming here. It was considered a sacred haven to the tribe Kaylana was part of. She brought me here because she thought this was the place one of their gods had captured the stars in. We are safe. You stopped bleeding a long time ago."

She nodded and dug into the bag, looking for the pants that she pulled out earlier. When she did, she laid out what he had brought back. Most were the bits of metal from her ship that she might be able to use, and there were a couple of instruments from her ship. She held them up in the little light she had. One of them was part of her communications system. It was an integral part she might be able to use. From everything she had heard and read about Earth, their science was still in its infancy. She picked up the battered part and poked at the frayed ends with the exposed wires.

"Can you use that?"

A sigh slipped from her lips. "I think so, but I'm going to need more equipment to get it going. Do you have the things you took from the encampment? Or any tools?"

"You were being attacked. I threw the bag into a tree. I was going back to retrieve it tonight."

Disappointment and fear filled Alika. She did not want Phillip to get hurt or captured because of her. He had already uprooted his domicile so the government would not catch her. Now he had to put himself in jeopardy again to retrieve the instruments he had stolen. "I can't ask you to go back and risk being captured. I won't let you go." She got up and paced. He touched her shoulder. His claws scraped against her flesh, but she knew it was supposed to be gentle by the emotions that rolled through his mind. There was also conflict too because he did not want to leave her, but he also wanted to make sure she got done what she needed to.

"You know I have to go back. You need the computer so you can you use it to send out a distress call. I'll be okay." He curled his fingers along her cheek and ran his thumb over her bottom lip. She turned her cheek into his palm and stared into his deep brown eyes. She saw the compassion and the man inside of him and knew that he was going to go no matter what she said.

"At least let me…"

He shook his head. *"No. You're staying here. Promise me."*

She nodded.

"Good. I'll be back."

He backed away from her and then slipped into the darkness, leaving the cave without a sound; even she could not detect him.

While he was gone, she went through his pants and the bag. She found some wrapped food in the bottom of the bag, sniffed it, and decided that it was edible. It tasted more like sand, but it was something to stop her stomach from growling. Alika then found something wrapped in a brown wrapper with silver clinging to it. She broke into it to find that it was quite appealing. After she finished the treat, she laid down on the sleeping bag. Stars shone brightly through the holes in the ceiling. Some of them she could name, but others were some she had not seen. They all made her homesick.

Alika did not know how long she stared, but she heard a shuffle and sat up in bed. A large shadow moved, and Phillip appeared in the cave. The sky was cresting with the golds and oranges of the sun coming onto the horizon. The man before her bellowed and dropped to his knees. A bag was slung over his shoulders. As he fell, his form shrunk and became the man he truly was.

In the light, she could make out scrapes and scratches along his flesh. He did not move except to remove the bag from over his shoulder, hand it to her, and then crawl into the sleeping bag that she had been sitting on. Phillip's back was all gouged up. *Maybe he was in a fight with another animal.* It appeared that his left leg was hurt because dried blood streaked down it. She went over to him.

"Are you okay?" she asked.

He forced a smile, but she noticed the pain in his eyes. "I'll be fine. Don't worry about me. The wounds will heal. I'm doomed to live eternally…"

She ran her fingers over his leg, and he winced when she came to his knee. Something had happened to Phillip. She grabbed the water and tore off a piece of the shirt she wore. Alika used the water and the fabric to clean the wound. When that happened, he grimaced and howled in pain. The intensity of it flashed through her mind, and she knew that he was only putting her off. When the wound was cleaned, she discovered something lodged in his knee. *If I had my ship, this would not be a problem.* "Griqnak…"

Phillip started laughing.

"What?" she snapped, not seeing what was so amusing.

"I assume that's some kind of curse in your language because I didn't get the translation."

Alika smiled. "Yes. It is also related to coupling, a very crude form of it."

"We have one like that too. It's called fuck."

"F-f-fu-ck." Alika wrapped her tongue around the strange syllables and found the sound and the weight of the word on her lips pleasing.

"Yes." Phillip sucked in a large breath when she took off her shirt and tied it around the wound to staunch the bleeding.

"You can walk. So what happened to you?"

"I retrieved the bag, and one of the army guys caught me jumping down from the tree. They called for backup and chased me through the woods. Even with my abilities, it was troublesome to lose them. Sometimes not even the power to cloak my presence can hide a seven-and-a-half-foot-tall creature if they're looking hard enough. I tried to go back through the entrance of the cave, but it was swarming with soldiers. So I had to take the long away around. I finally lost them. When I jumped down from a ledge, I landed wrong and broke my tibia. It pierced my skin. It has already started to heal. Don't worry; accelerated healing goes with part of who I am."

Alika ran her fingers over the place where the bone had broken. She pressed the flesh, and he jumped. The bone had already set into place. Healing was not one of her specialties. There were other positions on her planet that focused on the healing arts. She was more of a scout to seek out other life forms and evaluate whether they were compatible with their species. Earth had been far from her list. Phillip bellowed when she pressed on it again.

"Stop. Please!"

An idea hit her when she saw the pain in his eyes and the sweat dripping from his brow. She ran her fingers over his cheek, feeling the bone structure, and pressed the center of his forehead where the implant was. He began to speak, but she placed a finger over his lips. Alika focused on the circular piece of metal and the subtle ridges along it. Small tendrils stayed embedded in Phillip's flesh. The main apparatus glowed a subtle green when she pressed along the outer edge. Sometimes the translator could be used to ease pain. There was a built-in pain inhibitor that could last a few hours if used as a last resort. She just had to remember what buttons to push. After she slid her fingers around the translator, it glowed orange and then green again. Alika poked Phillip's leg by the bandage; he did not jump or flinch. She smiled and pushed the translator back into the middle of his forehead.

"Do you feel any pain now?"

Phillip shook his head. His warm hands cupped her face. The small gesture ignited the lust inside of her. This time it was not for the rushed encounter she had with him as a Bigfoot, but to be with the man inside. Phillip took in a deep breath and slid his hands down her sides. The smooth gesture made her squirm. She breathed in his masculine scent and also caught the musk that was part of the beast. Her hearts beat double time with the slight touch, and she was aroused even more than she had been with him as a beast. It was a strange sensation because she had not felt anything similar since her original mate had died.

"You never answered my question. Are you in pain now?"

Phillip pushed a stray hair from her face. "No pain. I'm just realizing how amazing you are. The light plays off your skin, and the way the crystals flash across your face makes you so ethereal."

Alika was not sure what the last word meant, but from his tone of voice and expression she assumed that he was a little mad. She reached up to touch the center of his forehead again and adjust his translator. Phillip caught her wrist.

"No, it has nothing to do with the device you implanted in my head. Being a Bigfoot, there are things I feel that I can't put into words. While I am a man, there are other things that I yearn to say. It's been so long since I've felt something for another person, since I've had someone real to talk to. It puts things into perspective."

She felt the sides of her cheeks sear at what he had said. If someone else had found her besides him, she did not know what she would have done. *He probably would have sold me off to the highest bidder.* "Phillip, you have no obligation to me. You've gone beyond any bond of chivalry or debt you think you owe me. I'm the one who is in your debt. You saved my life and risked yours on more than one occasion for me when you didn't have to." Alika forced a smile and stared into his brown eyes. For the first time, she considered not calling for help and maybe settling down with Phillip. *Maybe I could make a life here. Maybe I could learn to fit in on this planet. He cares for me, but could I stay here?*

"You are worth all the time and all the risks. I wish..." He shook his head.

She saw the unfinished thought flash across his face and in his mind. Normally, his thoughts were guarded while he was in his human form. This time Alika caught the depth of his emotions. Alika pressed her lips to his and did not bother with rational thought any longer. It was easier just to let her feelings take over. It was wonderful just to be able to feel and not think. There was no need to run. She could just be with Phillip, and he made her feel as if she were truly the only one in the universe. Phillip returned the kiss with a hunger that reflected his yearning for her. It was clear that he was lonely from all the time he had spent by himself.

"Are you sure you want to do this?" Phillip broke the kiss.

A cold chill passed down Alika's spine. She wondered why he was asking her when clearly he desired her. "Of course I wish to do this. Unless you don't."

He chuckled. "Oh, I do, but I thought you might enjoy it more if I was a Bigfoot. I'm average like this."

She understood now. All men, no matter what species, were enthralled with their manliness. Alika trailed her fingers over the firmness of his chest downward until she cupped his cock. "There is nothing average about you."

Phillip's lips spread into a wide smile. From there he laid his hand over her breast. His thumb brushed over her nipple. It hardened. A moan slipped from her lips, and her stomach quivered with anticipation. Phillip's lips slid over her throat, and his other hand slithered up her inner thigh. A giggle tumbled up her chest, and she squirmed.

"You're ticklish." Phillip nibbled her throat.

She nodded. "We call it something else."

Phillip ran his nose along the side of her neck. "What do you call it?"

His musky scent enveloped her. "Vgfyrin."

"Vgfyr..."

Alika knew that he tried to say it the way she did but he swallowed the last of the word, garbling it. Phillip tried again, but she pressed her fingers to his lips. He flicked his tongue over her fingertips. He sucked in one finger and then wrapped his tongue around it. Her hearts sped up, and her breath caught in her throat. She gripped his thigh and squeezed. Phillip released her finger and nipped her neck.

His fingers subtly pushed against her legs to open them further. Alika fought against it at first. What was it that he had in mind? Did he truly know how to pleasure her? Was he going to try and titillate her?

"Lie back," Phillip urged.

"But you don't know..."

"Shh...let me savor you." The ache in his voice tugged on her heart.

Alika closed her eyes and laid back. His lips swept over hers in the lightest kiss as he planted more along her throat and chest, taking a moment to lick her stomach and stopping at the bottoms she wore. His eyes glistened with excitement and anticipation. Her stomach was alight with trepidation. He slowly pulled down her bottoms, taking one leg at a time until she was completely naked. Phillip kissed the top of her feet and flicked his tongue over the top of her six toes. She squirmed again.

"Ticklish again?"

She shook her head. "No. I'm all dirty, but you don't seem to mind."

Phillip flashed a smile at her. "Dirt doesn't bother me. All I see is your beautiful body."

Alika's cheek seared at his compliments. Some of the males she had been with in the past had been fastidious about cleanliness. Others wanted her just in her animal form. Even though she had lost her mate ages ago, this was her first time with another male. She felt loved and wanted. Her lover straddled her. His fingers trailed up her calves, and his light touch stroked her inner thighs. His teeth replaced the lips on her leg. Phillip bit down on her skin. Alika arched off the sleeping bag and screamed. Wetness gushed from her pussy. He pressed his fingers into her hips while his body nestled between her legs. Kisses trailed from her abdomen until he found her buried clit. Once his lips encompassed her throbbing bud, a groan loosened from her throat.

Phillip slipped a finger inside of her depths and pushed against the sensitive walls. She raised her hips, trying to set a pace for their coupling. Phillip continued to pump into her and then added another finger while his tongue flicked over her clit, manipulating her faster and faster. The pleasure she experienced burned her to the core. Her canis form struggled to be let out, but she kept it in check. A cry left her throat that was part scream, part howl. Her hearts hammered against her chest. He was driving her into a frenzy, coaxing her higher and higher until it seemed that she would join the stars. Her skin burned from the passion he instilled in her. White light appeared behind her eyes. It grew brighter and brighter, increasing with the ecstasy he imparted into her.

He drove his fingers deeper into her until he had three fingers inside of her pussy. Phillip stroked her clit with fierceness as he redoubled his efforts. Alika tried to focus on her breathing to slow down the rising tide that would sweep her away, but it was nearly impossible not to give in.

"P-please," Alika pleaded.

Phillip didn't relent. She ran her fingers over his muscled arms and slipped them over his shoulders. She raked her nails along his spine, and it did not deter him. No man had ever driven her crazy the way he was doing to her. Alika writhed under him. Sweat had broken out on her skin. She was so close to ecstasy, all that was needed to send her over the edge was a small push. And Phillip gave her that little nudge when he nibbled on her clit once more and then trailed his tongue along her moist slit, replacing his fingers with his tongue. Once he did, Alika cried out and felt her muscles lock up as stars burst in her mind. Her pleasure flooded her and she basked in the glory.

Her lover didn't stop delving into her pussy. Instead, Phillip kept on torturing her until only choked gasps left her throat. It was not until a second wave of delight picked her up and carried her away that he relented. Alika tried to catch her breath. Her hearts jackhammered into her ribcage. Phillip's smile beamed down at her. He leaned over and kissed her so that she tasted her nectar on him.

"Did you enjoy that?" he asked.

She nodded, still trying to catch her breath. "Very much. Where did you learn such a skill?"

Phillip kissed her cheek and snaked his fingers lower, but she grabbed his hand before he could start manipulating her again. She was not sure if she could handle another session with him. Besides, she wanted a chance to pleasure him too.

"I have my secrets."

"You would make a wonderful asset on my planet. The women would *love* you."

"I'll just stick to you."

Alika smiled and slipped her hand down his length. Phillip shimmied down her body. She stroked him until he squirmed and moaned. Feeling the firmness of his prick, she yearned to have him inside of her.

"Where did you learn that?"

Alika grinned. "Most males have sexual organs such as yours. And I learn to adapt. I want you inside of me."

He kissed her deeply, and she felt him plumping up even more. She cupped his balls and squeezed. His eyes rolled back, and he thrust his hips into her hand. Alika slipped her hand around his neck and brought him down on top of her. She reached down and eased his cock into her. Alika groaned as his prick moved into her. It felt so right, and this time she did not have to switch her shape to accommodate him.

"You feel so good."

Phillip clutched her breasts and squeezed her nipples. She cried out. He kissed her shoulders, and his hot breath blasted against her throat. He pinched her nipples harder. The pain sent bolts of sensation to her clit. Phillip's heavy breathing filled her ears. With her eyes shut, Alika lost herself in the tempo of their lovemaking. The bliss surged through her. Her man was building her to another peak that would rocket her to another world. Screams echoed in the cave. She barely recognized them for her own. Phillip pounded into her harder. He groaned and then slid into her one final time. She felt him release inside of her. He rested his head on her chest for a second and slid his fingers from her breasts. From there he touched her clit.

"What are you doing?" she asked, pulling in her breath.

He did not answer her but began to rub her once again. Alika cried out from the swiftness of the delight that captured her. Phillip drove into her a couple more times, heightening their experience together. He continued to fondle her until he brought her down and she was out of breath. Then they collapsed onto the sleeping bag together.

Chapter Seven

Phillip awoke from the most restful sleep he had had in a long time. It seemed almost as if it was some bad dream in which he had become a monster and when he was waking up it was to the woman he had loved. He stretched and looked around him. It all rushed back. Kaylana was no longer with him, but he had fallen asleep in the arms of another woman, a very sexy and beautiful green-skinned woman who had come from outer space to be with him. Although Phillip wanted her to stay, after the debacle with the army the day before, they would never stop looking for her. Hell, they could be swarming the caves now, searching for signs of them. It was a mistake to get photographed. But there was nothing he would not do to keep her secure. Alika was not safe on this planet. No matter how much she could try to fit in, her unusual skin coloring and the fact that she turned into a wolf sometimes would force her to stand out. It was not fair to make her live underground when there was a vast world she could explore. He knew many hidden places where he had traveled, and since he had transformed he preferred the mountains.

Ever since he first saw the rising peaks in the New World, Phillip had fallen in the love with the tribes. Since Kaylana had died, he had spent his years traversing across the Americas, Canada, and had walked into South America learning some of the secrets of the tribes there. They had been the most welcoming, even in his other form, and had revered him. From there he had gone up the West Coast and into Alaska, keeping to the dense forest. One thing he discovered while in Alaska, where they had hours and days of sun, was that he could remain a man. It was during this time that he had rowed with the local people to the Diomede Islands between the straits and then over to Russia. From there he had gone all over, but never made it into Western Europe because it was too populated, and never into the desert because he would not be able to hide. In the end, Phillip returned to the Appalachian Mountains. Even now there were people encroaching on his home, and soon he wondered if he would have to live forever in a cave. He could deal with the blight that had been laid upon him, but he never did want to bring that upon Alika. She deserved better.

He ran his fingers over the sleeping bag and found a warm spot. However, she was not with him. A momentary stab of worry went through him, but he trusted Alika. So Phillip unwound the bandage from his leg and the now healed bone. There was one thing about his blight that he appreciated. Of course, it was all part of the shaman's plan for him to live for all eternity. Phillip had tried various ways of ending his existence in the early years of his curse. Nothing worked; it just caused him pain. Eventually, he stopped trying. With the way the weapons were today, he wondered if in the event that he was blown to bits whether his body would reconstruct itself from those small particles or if he would finally have true peace. Right now he yearned to spend whatever time he could with Alika, no matter how short that time was. At last he stood, found a back part of the cave to relieve himself, then dug into the backpack for another power bar to ease the hollow ache in his stomach. Eventually, he would have to go out for more supplies. Living off the cardboard-tasting food bars was not his original idea. It would be better if he hunted and brought down game. For a second, he entertained hunting with Alika in her wolf form. She was a glorious sight with two tails and six toes on each foot, which gave her a uniqueness that he would always envy. He figured that they would make great hunting partners.

"I was wondering when you'd be waking up."

Phillip stared into her beautiful orange eyes. For a moment, he forgot she had said something and felt his neck burning. "Well, you took a lot out of me earlier." Alika looked enticing in the too-tight jeans that hugged her body and the white tank top that showed off the swells of her breasts. Her dark green nipples were visible through the thin fabric. The thought of making love to her again hardened his cock. He wrapped his arms around her and pulled her close, nuzzling her neck. Phillip placed kisses along the line of her throat. She moaned and then pressed against him.

"I want you again," he whispered in her ear.

Alika placed a hand on his chest and pushed him away. Her eyes were dilated with pleasure, and she was breathing heavily. Her restraint seemed to be slipping. "Even though I do enjoy coupling with you, I have to see if I can make a transmitter out of the instruments you thieved for me."

"Are you having any luck?" Phillip asked. He smoothed his hair back and tried to think of other things than Alika's lithe body so he would not have to suffer the terrible throbbing he was dealing with in his dick.

She sighed. "Not so well. Come here, I'll show you what I've done."

Phillip saw where she had carefully laid out the computer, the cell phone, and the bits he had taken from the equipment he had stolen from the army encampment. He was also glad he had thought to grab some of the tools lying around. The pliers were the main tool she was using. The laptop was split open and the hard drive removed. The cell phone was also in pieces, and the bits she had from her ship remained separate.

"What else do you need?" he asked.

"I need some kind of a power source. I can use the crystals, but I need a way to harness their power. The computer parts are great, but I need…" She looked around at the parts and shook her head. "I need more than what you have here. I hate to say it, but I must go to a place where there are electronics available. Then I can tell what I need."

He heard the desperation in her voice. They both knew that she needed to go home. He glanced at the sky. The sun would set in a few hours. The cave system went a few more miles and connected with old mine shafts close to town. However, he hated to venture that way because sections of the mine shafts were unstable. If they left now, they could make it to the mines. Then under the cover of darkness, they could go into town and get what Alika needed.

He nodded. "There's probably a place in town, an electronics store or general store, that will have what you need. If we go now, we can reach the mines and weave through them until we get to the edge of town. After that, we have to wait for darkness and when the place closes down."

Her face lit up. "That'd be great. Of course, we will be careful in the tunnels. We'll look out for one another."

"Yes, we will. Let me put some clothes on and pack the bag. We'll need it later. I'm afraid I don't have any shoes or hiking boots for you."

Her brow creased as she tried to figure out what he said. Phillip pointed to his feet. "Boots are coverings we wear on our feet to protect them or to keep our feet warm."

She nodded. "Okay, I understand now. We have the same thing, but all of my garments went up with my ship. Clothes are cumbersome when I change forms."

Phillip chuckled. "I know how you feel. I always try to leave my clothes in a place where they won't be disturbed while I'm a Bigfoot. Over the years, that hasn't always worked."

She slid her fingers over his chest. "I prefer you in your own flesh without the fabric covering you, but I understand the necessity for it. Not all cultures are two-natured, and many have rules or taboos about being unclothed." Her nails scraped over his nipple. "I'm sure you've seen many different things in your travels."

"More than you know." She placed a kiss on his cheek as her nails dug into his pecs. Alika pierced his flesh painlessly, and that made his dick firm once more.

"You keep doing that, and we won't be going anywhere." He took her hands and guided them away from his chest.

"I can't help it. Something about you appeals to me more than any other male I have been with. But yes, you're right, you need to get dressed and we should go."

Phillip pulled on an old pair of jeans and a T-shirt. He didn't have any boots either anymore, so it was a barefoot trip for him too. Dressed and packed, he took a lantern and motioned for Alika to follow. He led them back to the waterfall. The spray hit him, and the image of Alika naked under the spray in a sun-filled pool flashed through his mind. For a moment the blood left his brain, but he forced himself to think about the journey ahead. Phillip slipped behind a narrow opening to the left of the waterfall and held out his light so Alika could see. The first part of their trek was not so perilous. When the earth was looser under his feet and the aroma of the air grew damper, they knew that they were close to the mines. Animals scurried out of their way and spiderwebs hit him in the face, clinging to his skin. Drips of sweat were streaming down his face by the time he stopped. He dug into his bag and pulled out a bottle of water, took a few sips, then handed the rest to Alika. She smiled at him and took the bottle.

"Is it much farther?" she asked.

"We're at the end of the mines now, toward the back of a couple of the shafts. They used to dig for silver here, but after a big disaster almost two hundred years ago, they abandoned the mines. Tales say that the shafts are haunted by the spirits of those who died here."

"Is that what you believe?" Alika finished the water and passed him back the empty bottle.

He thought about the ghost stories he had heard over the years and the things he had seen. Even in the old mine, he had witnessed some things. "I believe that there are some people who don't pass on, and they get stuck behind in a certain place. I don't know. Come on. It will be dark soon; I can feel the weight of the sun settling on my shoulders and don't want to be caught in the tight spots when I'm over seven feet tall."

She nodded. "I agree."

The light from his flashlight beamed into the darkness and split the shadows. Once in a while he caught a pair of eyes that reflected the light. The load-bearing beams creaked. He hardly dared touch them in case they might splint and break. He was surprised that they had lasted this long, but he doubted that anyone had ventured into the mines for days unless they were teenagers searching for a thrill. He treaded carefully. When he arrived at a branch in the tunnels, he stopped and had to remember which way to go. It was getting harder to breathe. A cool breeze slid by the side of his face, so he followed it to the left. As he walked a few steps, the floor gave way beneath him. The light fell from his hand and rolled back toward Alika. A gasp left his lips, and he felt himself falling. Panic overwhelmed him. If he fell he would live, but he was not sure if he would be able to climb out. He could not risk anything happening to Alika. As his fingers grasped on to the remains of a wooden floorboard, he felt his grip slipping.

"Phillip, stay where you are!" Alika called down to him.

"No, stay there. The floor is too weak. I don't want you to fall too."

Her head appeared above him. She shone the light down and stretched her arm out so he could grab on to it. When he reached up, the bag slipped from his shoulder. He tried to take hold of it, but it fell and landed somewhere at the bottom of the shaft. "Forget about the bag. Give me your hand."

His heart jumped into his throat. The sun was setting. His bones were already taking on extra weight. It was only a matter of time before he would change completely. "I'm too heavy. You won't be able to pull me up."

She stretched her arm further into the hole, dangling precariously close to the edge. Her fingertips brushed his wrist. "I'm stronger than I look. Now give me your hand!"

Phillip extended his arm and felt his fingernails growing. He was changing. His muscles were taking on bulk. Tonight, with all of his being, he fought the transformation coming over him. Alika grabbed a hold of his hand. In the light he saw that her eyes had changed color, and her arms seemed to be longer. He ran his tongue over his teeth and felt that they were sharper. Phillip grasped on to her arm, and she hauled him to the top of the hole until he could get a good grip on the lip. With one fierce tug, she wrenched him over the side of the pit. They both rolled toward the wall. The muscles in his body expanded. His ribs cracked and rearranged; a couple more appeared in order to support the great weight of his chest. Phillip's spine elongated and popped. Phillip howled with pain. The more he fought it, the longer it seemed to take. He felt Alika's hands on his forehead trying to soothe his pain, but it was like this every night, the shaman's way of punishing him for feeling the same pain that he felt when he lost his daughter. Phillip's sentence was an eternal damnation of turning into a hairy creature and never finding true happiness.

"Breathe, Phillip. Let the change flow through you. Embrace it, and there will be no pain."

"That's...easy...for you...to sayyy!" His words turned into a howl. At first he jerked away from Alika and gnashed his teeth at her, not recognizing her. It was always like this when he changed because it took him a minute to orient. Each night the beast in him seemed to steal away another shred of his humanity. Phillip wondered if he would one day succumb to the beast, and he would cease to exist. The animal sensed something about Alika, something like kinship and something else. Something of an ownership that Phillip could not quite understand. As he stared into Alika's eyes, he saw her lips moving and tried to speak, finally pushing the animal out of his mind and back into his cage. He then was able to focus on the woman before him.

"Are you okay?" she asked.

He stood up and stretched, feeling the power coursing through his body. *"Yes. I am okay now. Thanks."*

"Why do you fight your transformation?"

Anger welled up in him, and he could not grab a hold of it. He turned his claws into a fist and slammed it into the wall, showering dust over them. He bared his teeth and placed his other hand on her cheek. When Phillip touched her, a sense of calm washed over him. Being close to Alika helped him concentrate when he was hairy, and he was not sure why. *"I fight it because I always have. This was never a gift given to me. Your wolf shape seems to be your natural state. It's not that way with other humans. We don't share your ability. This form is my punishment."*

"For the one who lies under the stones?"

He nodded. *"Yes. For her. So that I'd know her father's pain of losing her."*

"There are places on my planet where the night does not fall. Surely your curse wouldn't follow you if there is no night."

"Correct. There was a time when I traveled north and found a place where the sun did not set. I was a man for as long as the sun was up. It lasted a couple of months and allowed me to cross the ocean. I slept and woke as me. My plight is associated with the rising and setting of the sun."

"Maybe you should think about going back there or maybe coming with me."

Phillip shook his head. *"Come on, we need to get through the rest of these tunnels."*

Alika tried to respond but he walked past her, stopping to pick up the light, not wanting to think about the road ahead or the glimmer of hope that lived inside of his heart.

Chapter Eight

Alika sensed the conflict inside of Phillip when she mentioned him coming with her, but she did not bring it up. Instead, she concentrated on where she stepped until they finally emerged from the darkness into the night where the stars seemed buried within the thick clouds. She smelled moisture on the air. It would soon rain. She hoped it would happen quickly so she could wash some of the grime off. It was good to be outside in the cool air. Being underground, it seemed that the walls were coming closer and about to collapse on her. Even though the cave was underground, there were holes in the ceiling to see the stars, and it was spacious enough to feel as if she were still free. Phillip led her through the forest until they were at the edge of a human settlement. It was difficult to concentrate the longer she was around Phillip. Her mind should have been focused on the implements she needed to create the communication device she had to assemble. Mainly, she needed a power source and some other tools. Alika's thoughts lingered on their coupling and how magnificent he had made her feel with his hands and his tongue. It was one of the most satisfying experiences she had ever had with any lover, and she yearned to have him again.

Time passed, and the town came into view. At last, the shadows seemed to be long enough that Phillip motioned for them to get going. They stayed to the dark part of the streets and flattened against buildings in case someone drew near. While she was close to Phillip, she sensed some power around him that she could not explain. When she pulled away from him, she saw that it was darker around him; the shadows concealed and almost made him blend in so it was harder to determine that he was there. It was an interesting trick, and she wondered if she could master the technique.

They got to the rear of a building, and Phillip stood by the door. *"Do you know what you're going to get?"*

"I have an idea of what I need. I just need to see it."

"Stay here. I will disable their alarm system." He walked around the corner. The light blinked off. Phillip returned and opened the door. *"I don't know how much time we will have, so we have to be quick."*

"That was my plan anyway."

He ducked inside of the building. Alika followed behind him. Inside were all kinds of wares that distracted her. Labeled cylinders with pictures of what appeared to be food lined the shelves. She shook herself from her daze and found that Phillip had taken a bag. He went to a tall black case with beverages inside of it and placed them inside of the bag.

"We'll need more water. The electronics are here. There isn't much, I'm afraid. This is the general store and has only few things. This way."

He led her to an aisle that had some things she might need. She spied a large bag that was similar to what Phillip had lost and took it. She glanced around and saw a primitive-looking battery she might be able to use. Something reflective caught her eye.

"You have a battery for a power source and a space blanket. Do you need anything else?"

She quickly ran through the ingredients she had in her bag. "Wire. I think that might be it."

A large crash echoed where Phillip moved to. She figured that something had fallen. He reappeared with a spool of copper wire and threw it into her bag. *"You look around and see if there's anything else you want. I'm going to get more water and some food."*

Alika nodded and quickly hurried through the store, coming upon a shelf that had several of those dark brown-labeled bars that she had enjoyed before. She scooped what she could into her bag and then added a few more just to be on the safe side. They might not be considered food, but they were heavenly. They would make a great birthday gift for Elarna. She glanced around and saw some garments. Phillip appreciated having her clothed, so she took some of those too.

Outside she heard shouts arising from the street. Peering out the window, she saw figures approaching with lights bobbing, running toward the store. They must have realized that they had entered it.

"Phillip, humans are coming. We have to get out of here."

"I know. Follow me." He tapped her shoulder.

She had not even realized that he was behind her. Alika moved with him through the store, clutching her full bag. They made it outside in the darkness, and the voices were getting louder. They were inside the building. Phillip pressed her back against the wall. The power emanating from him also enveloped her. One of the humans rushed past them, and he did not see them. Alika held her breath and quieted the beating of her two hearts. The male took a moment and then returned out of breath.

"I don't see anyone," he called to someone inside of the store.

"They have to be around here somewhere."

"Yo, Donald, you're not going to believe this! Come in and take a look at the size of these footprints!"

The man stared straight at them. Alika just knew he would see them, but he did not. Instead, he slipped into the shop and did not come back out. She still held her breath as Phillip took her hand and led her through the darkness back to the mine. They heard footsteps and twigs breaking as they neared the entrance to the mine. Phillip held her against the trees. So far they were hidden, but she was not sure how long that would last.

"They found us," she whispered.

Phillip glanced at her and put a finger to his muzzle. She glanced at the stars and thought she saw something moving, floating above the foliage. Footsteps ricocheted through the night, but did not draw closer. Who or what was it? Phillip gestured that it was time to move, so she did. They made it to the entrance of the mines when a large light appeared out of nowhere from the sky and shone down on them. Both of them froze.

"Stop where you are!" a voice commanded from above.

Alika glanced up and saw a man leaning over the edge of the flying machine with a rifle pointed at them, hovering very close above them, and she had not heard them. They must have had some stealth technology. This planet was surprising her more and more. She glanced at Phillip. "What do we do?"

He growled and dropped the bag, moving her behind him. *"Whatever happens, stay behind me. If I get hurt, I will heal. When you get the chance, run into the mines. Make it back to the caves. Build your machine and get out of here."*

Alika realized that he was going to sacrifice himself for her. He touted that he was immortal and no matter what injury he got he would heal, but she did not know that. There was no way she was going to let him put himself in harm's way. "No." She jumped out from behind him and pushed him back. "I'm not going to let you do anything. You can hide yourself from them, can't you?"

"Yes, but I'm not sure whether they can see me or not."

"It doesn't matter. We're in this together. I'm faster on four legs than two. If you can carry my bag, we can distract them. I'll run them off in another direction. They won't suspect it."

He growled, showing her his teeth. Alika sensed that he wasn't happy about the plan, but before he could say anything she shoved her bag at him and stripped off her clothes. The light was still on them. She did not care anymore if they saw her shift. Alika stared into the light and caressed her breasts because of the males she had met; they all seemed to be fascinated with that part of her anatomy. The light moved a little and followed her. Her bones moved and popped, but she welcomed the shift rather than fight it the way Phillip did. It flowed through her until she was down on all fours. Then she took off into the woods. Phillip howled in frustration. The light did not follow her.

She slunk into the shadows and ran toward the mountains. Not sure of where she was going, she raced away from town and human habitation. It was better for all of them. As the elevation rose higher, she caught a familiar scent. It was the faint scent of exhaust from her ship and the aroma of charred earth. The tops of the trees were burned away where her ship had sheared them and made a clear path, giving her a trail to follow. Alika tried to stay far away from it but still follow it, until she came to the place where her ship had crashed. There was no human presence to speak of. The army had moved off. It was almost as if they had not been there at all because they had left no footprints. The area was empty except for the grass and the trees. They had cleared out and gathered all of her ship parts. Taking a minute, she sniffed the air and did not sense any humans. Carefully she went into the crash site and nosed around in the dirt, hoping to find something left of her vessel.

After finding nothing, Alika went in the direction where she was thrown. She prayed she might find something of her ship near the rocks where she had headed after the crash.

While she scoured the ground, she saw something glint from the starlight. Alika transformed back to human form and pushed the rocks out of the way. Down in the hole, she pulled out the very thing she needed. It was the size of the cell phones Phillip had taken for her case. It had been on her belt when she had left the ship. After that Alika did not remember what had happened to it or her clothes, just that she had transformed. Her body had tried to keep itself alive, and she had gone into shock.

She opened the pouch and prayed that it was still working. When she touched the silver screen, it blinked on. A sigh of relief flooded through her system. It was more than just a communicator. It contained preloaded star charts just in case the main computer went down in the ship; she would be able to use it in a pinch, and there was a long-range communicator built into it too. In the distance, she could see the light from the flying machine that the military had. That meant that Phillip had led them away or they had broken off their search for him and decided to come looking for her. She glanced at the darkness and knew that the entrance to the caves was not far off, but she did not want to chance it in case the military remained. Instead, she thought about getting higher. It would have been nice to have had a form that could take to the air, but her kind only had one animal form. Sometimes they were flyers, but most of the time they were four-legged.

I can't stay here. I really need to get back to the caves we were at before, and I don't know how to do that. If I can get to the gravesite then, maybe there is someplace there that I can hide. I have to risk it. Alika placed the device on the ground and slipped back into her canis form. Then she grabbed it carefully between her teeth and followed her nose. She caught Phillip's faint scent still clinging to the grass and ran along it until she was at the gravesite again. Alika did not smell any other humans that had disturbed the area, so she assumed that it was safe. Back in human form, she pressed a few buttons on the communicator and it whirred to life. She tapped the screen to open a star chart that showed Rovan. An image of her planet popped up. Alika tapped a few more places on the screen, and a loud beep issued from the device. It was sending out the signal. All she hoped was that it would get there.

It was not going to happen overnight, but she could wait. And with the tools they had gotten, she could boost the signal. It would work. It had to. She took the communicator and held it against her chest. Alika found a niche in the mountain wall and sat with her back against the stone. The hardness kept her anchored. If the message did not reach Rovan, then she was going to be stuck on Earth. She certainly could not do it as a woman. Maybe as a wolf she could find some unpopulated wilderness and settle down. But if she could live with Phillip, then she could deal with her life on Earth.

The sun rose, streaking across the horizon in various shades of gold and pink. It was very different from the deep purples and crimsons that accompanied the dawn on her world. Small flying creatures began to tweet in the bushes around her. The chill of the night had worn off, and she felt the warmth of the dawn on her skin. Phillip had not returned. She was worried and prayed that nothing had happened to him. After waiting for several more hours, the shadows were no longer concealing her. The only place for her to wait was in the cave. Hopefully, the military had not set any traps in the cavern. She remembered the path to the backside of the cave and slid inside of it. Alika did not smell any human presence as she walked toward the main cave where she and Phillip had first stayed. Human scent permeated the small space. Everything that had been sacred to Phillip was scattered about and other stuff was removed. What would they find in his books and clothing? She found a torn-up sleeping bag and curled up in the remnants of it. From there, she found sleep.

When she woke up, it was dark out and there was still no sign of Phillip. A spear of disappointment struck her heart, along with fear. The longer he was gone, the more she wondered if she would see him again. Had he been captured? Was she ever going to feel his touch again? She rooted around in the remains of things and found some more of the wrapped bars that she had before and ate them. They filled the hollow in her stomach, but not in her heart. She picked up a few of the volumes lying about and tried to read the words. It was all gibberish to her. The translator was not set to interact with her optical nerves. She did find one that had pictures in it. Some of them reminded her of the objects she had seen around the mountain. Others appeared to be plants, and some were avian creatures that flew through the air. Others were similar landscapes on other planets, and there were a few unique to Earth. Many of the scenes were beautiful. The images displayed frozen mountains and beasts. She checked her computer and saw that the signal was still going. She was not sure how long the power source would last. It would be best if she could find the crystals she had in the other cave. Then she could harness the energy.

Alika flipped through the book again and then walked around. As the night wore on, she found another bottle of water and ate the bars sparingly. All her thoughts were about the time she had spent with Phillip. She found one of his discarded shirts and pressed it close to her nose, inhaling his masculine scent. It was then that she felt tears slip down her cheeks. She fell asleep clutching his shirt to her chest.

Her dreams were of them in one another's arms. Someone was holding her and murmuring in her ear. She opened her eyes and saw that she was in Phillip's arms. It was still night. She smiled when she saw him.

"I thought they captured you."

He brushed the hair from her eyes, and the caring reflected in his dark brown ones warmed her heart. *"I eluded them. There were a couple of close calls. I finally lost them a few hours ago. When I knew it was safe, I had to come back to you. Are you okay?"*

She nodded, threw her arms around his furry neck, and kissed his snout. It did not matter if he was a man or a beast. Alika knew that he was the man she wanted. There had to be some way she could convince him to come back with her. "I'm glad you came back. How did you find me?"

"I followed your scent from the crash site. I went by and saw that the humans had left. I wanted to be sure you were safe. They did a number on my cave."

"I found my communicator."

He brushed his claws down her cheek. *"I'm sure that's a relief to you. Do you still need all the items we collected?"*

"Yes. The signal is very weak, and I can hook this up to everything and actually send a message instead of a distress call. I did not know the way back to that particular cave."

Phillip lifted her up in his arms. *"Well, how about if we head back? There's no need to worry; I doubt the army is looking for us now."*

Alika sighed and hoped that that was the case. She felt more secure now that Phillip was back. She hugged him close, never wanting to let him go.

Chapter Nine

Phillip watched Alika assemble the communicator she was working on. It had taken a few hours for her to get everything the way she wanted. She had hooked it up to the crystals in the cave and was drawing power from them and from the battery. Also Alika had used the space blanket as an amplifier. He did not really understand the technology behind it, but she had used the wire he had gotten and connected it to the cell phone and the laptop. Her device had become the one thing in between each element. While she was working with the laptop, she downloaded the data onto her device and figured out what they had learned about her ship. There were pictures of her on the computer, of the trajectory of her vessel, and where it had entered the atmosphere. He glanced at the maps and at the point of entry. There were satellite images showing her ship coming into the atmosphere. They had gone through the information and there were blurry photos of him, but nothing concrete to show exactly what he was. It had taken her most of the night and into the morning to build the machine. Now they hoped that it would work the way she wanted it to.

"At least the signal is a lot stronger than what it was before. The power from the battery helped a lot. I was afraid that it was dying. I guess it was more damaged than I thought it was. Thank you for all your help."

"You're the one who put it together. I don't know what you did. It's not something I could build."

She stood on tiptoe to press her lips against his. As short as she was, she fit against his body in every way. Phillip never thought it would have been possible to love another woman the way he had loved Kaylana, but it was true. Over the short time they had known one another, Alika had become very dear to his heart. All he wanted was to protect her and keep her from going anywhere. He kissed her back and slid his tongue along her bottom lip, tasting a bit of the chocolate she had eaten earlier. Phillip had been surprised to find so many bars in her bag. He figured that when it came to chocolate, it seemed that even alien women had a taste for it. He pulled away from her and admitted that the T-shirt that hugged her body and the too-big jeans were enticing. They were belted with fabric that he had torn from another shirt. She looked scrumptious, and he wanted to eat her up.

"You would be able to build it. All those volumes you read, I'm sure you have read many things over the years."

"I read a lot and I know some offhand facts, a few languages from all over the world, and a few other things. I can carve and knit. I know how to make my own clothes. I can hunt for food, tan the hides of animals, and operate a gun if I need to. I have accumulated knowledge with the times, but I never got into really figuring out electronics. Living in caves and abandoned cabins where there is no electricity, there's no point for me to mess with computers much."

"That's understandable."

"So now that it's working, how long do you think it'll be before they come for you?"

Alika turned back toward the device and tapped it. The screen came on, and there were images of planets. She pressed the green planet, and a large picture came up. She punched the numbers on the laptop, and strange letters appeared on her clear screen.

"What are you typing? Why use only the numbers?" He was fascinated at what she was doing.

"I don't know your writing. Numbers are easy. They appear to be the same even in my language. The right combination of numbers, and I can spell a word. It takes time, but I've done it before. I'm sending a message of where we are. I got the coordinates from the laptop. That was a big help. I'm typing to let them know I'm alive and that someone is with me." She stopped typing and stared at him. He saw the hope in her eyes and knew what she was going to be asking him.

Phillip sighed and stared out of the hole in the cave ceiling. The sun was looming overhead, and he had been thinking over the same thing he knew that she was going to ask. "You want me to come with you?"

She glanced at the floor and then back at him. "I was hoping you would. On my planet you'd be treated like royalty. There would be many women who you could have in either form. They would pay you whatever you want. You…"

He placed a finger on her lips. "I don't want any other women. The only one I want is you."

"But you might have to help populate our planet and…"

"Alika, if that's something that comes up, then we shall deal with it."

"So you'll come with me?"

He nodded. "There's nothing for me here. And I don't want to leave you behind." He pushed the hair from her face and kissed her lightly.

"You know, I can help you with your bestial form. I can help you tame it, so you can call upon it anytime you wish."

"My transformation is a curse. I can't turn it off and on at will, not unless the sun sets or rises. I've tried. Because of it, my senses are enhanced, and I can pull on the powers of the elements when I'm human. Does it matter to you if I'm one or the other?"

"Of course not. I enjoy both of your forms." Her hand traveled down his chest and ran along the waistband of his jeans. "Do you want me to show you how much I enjoy them?" She slipped her hand below the fabric and touched his cock. At the first caress, he was already firm.

He smiled. "I'd love for you to show me."

Alika flashed him a wicked grin and unzipped his jeans. Phillip did not try to stop her, but was more intrigued at what she was going to do. She tugged his pants down around his hips, then pushed them lower until his dick sprang out. Then she slipped to her knees. Alika ran her tongue over the engorged shaft until Phillip groaned. She bit down gently before sucking his sensitive head into her mouth. She flicked her tongue along the length of the cock until she pulled the whole shaft into her mouth. Phillip moaned.

"Where did you learn to do that?"

She giggled and then sucked him slowly, twisting her tongue around his length until he could not hold back any longer. Phillip gripped the sides of her head, twining his fingers through her violet hair, and held Alika to him. He felt the beast inside of him rising. It was the first time he had felt the beast stir during the day, and he was not sure what to make of it. Before he could linger, Alika drew him all the way into her mouth. She raked her finger along his thighs, and with one hand squeezed his balls to keep him steady.

Phillip drew in a haggard breath. He was close to coming and felt that the beast was taking more control. He wanted to prolong the moment. The pleasure tightened his balls, and the animal inside of him growled with anticipation.

"That's it. Alika, oh God!"

Alika didn't stop, but kept sucking on his cock. Phillip thrust his hips into her face. His lover took his shaft between her lips one last time. The muscles contracted in his stomach. The animal inside of him roared. At that moment, he cried out and spilled his seed down Alika's throat. She grasped his balls one last time, rolling them in her hand before she released him and licked the remnants of his seed from his length. His breaths came in short pants as he tried to come back to himself, but the animal in him had not retreated. It had only come closer to him, sharing his body. He ran his tongue over his teeth, feeling their sharpness.

"Was that pleasing to you?"

Staring into her orange eyes, all he could do was nod. She trailed her fingers down his chest and pinched his nipple. He jumped, and a hiss fell from his lips. "I don't know what is happening to me."

She laid a hand over his heart and closed her eyes. A couple of seconds passed by; with each one he sensed his body taking on more mass. She opened her eyes. "You have connected with your inner Bigfoot. He wants to come out and play too."

"But I've never changed in the daylight."

"Have you ever tried?"

He shook his head. "No."

Alika stood on tiptoe and flicked her tongue over his lips. "Well, how about if we give it a try?"

Phillip thought about it. *What if I can access it? What would it be like? Why not?* He swept her up in his arms, which got her to squeal. The sound of her voice made him happy and hard once more. He deposited her on his sleeping bag. From there he planted kisses up her calf, moving along her soft skin to the bend of her knee, where Phillip bit lightly. Alika jerked her leg away. He gazed up at her.

"Sorry. Ticklish."

"It's okay. So how do we go about me controlling my inner Bigfoot?"

"Do you trust me?" Alika asked.

"Of course."

She arched up and kissed his lips. "Then lie back."

Phillip did as he was asked. They switched positions, and she straddled him. The beast stirred under his skin. It was also interested in this woman. Her gaze never left his as she slipped her hand behind her and gripped his shaft. A low growl rolled from his throat. It nearly caught him off-guard, and he was surprised at the gentle caress. Alika squeezed his balls until he squirmed. The pain that came from the gesture made him want her more. His muscles were taking on bulk. She placed her hand over his heart. It was beating faster.

"What now?"

She took one of his free hands and placed it on her chest. "Feel the beats of my hearts. You want to focus on breathing and matching your heartbeat to it. Once you do, then you can be in sync with your second form."

Phillip tried to do as his lover said. He tried to focus on feeling her heartbeats and his. But it was distracting because her flesh was so firm and her nipples so pert. He yearned to take one into his mouth and taste her flesh. His cock throbbed with the need of her. Although she was perched on top of him, his dick was so close to her wet slit that he could easily maneuver and be inside of her. He moved his hand and traced the curve of her right breast.

"No fair. That is not what I asked you to do."

"I can't help it. You feel so good." He lifted his hips and slid closer to her pussy.

Alika stretched over him until they were pressed together. "You make it hard for me to concentrate too, but try to breathe. Once you do that, then we can do so much more." She nibbled his bottom lip.

Phillip groaned. "Tease."

Alika nipped at his throat. Her teeth felt sharper. When she glanced up at him, her pupils were slits. It seemed that her face had taken on a different shape. It was leaner, and her face and nose protruded some. He reached up and trailed his finger over her cheek, feeling the different structure of her cheekbones. She snapped at his finger before flicking her tongue over the tip of it. Now her body seemed longer, but bulkier on top of him. He tried to focus on his breathing and not on the heat of her body. He closed his eyes while her tongue laved the side of his throat. The animal inside him howled to be let out. Her scent took on a musky undertone.

The change began to take him over, but it was coming too fast. His eyes snapped open, and he howled in pain. Alika kissed his throat, nipping and sucking at it.

"Calm yourself. Focus on my heart. Let it out slowly. That is how you take control," she said. Her words came out with a growl as though she was having trouble forming the words. He nodded and bit back another howl, trying to maintain control of his body.

Alika moved down his body only a little. He noticed that she was taller, and her body was now covered in a thin layer of brown fur. Even her purple locks had changed color. He laid his hand on her chest and felt her hearts. She slid down, took Phillip's prick, and slid it inside of her. He groaned at the tight fit. His lover moaned as he thrust inside of her. Phillip tried to ignore her and focus on the beats. As he did, he found the pain of his shifting body diminishing. If he concentrated on something else, it seemed that the Bigfoot in him came into his body more slowly.

"Yes," Alika gasped.

Phillip stared at the woman riding him. Her head was thrown back, and her eyes were shut. Her face was more animal with only a few human features. Her ears were pointed, and her nose and mouth had formed into a half-muzzle with canines curled over her lips. Her hands were sharp claws that pressed into his chest. It was an odd combination, but he found it all the more alluring. She opened her eyes, and her lips pulled back into a smile. At that moment, his beast took over and he lost control. The pain tore through him, but Alika began to ride him. The agony of the transformation blended with the pleasure of their coupling.

Alika rode him hard. As she did, he felt her tails brushing his legs. She did not balk at his length; instead, she seemed to enjoy his Bigfoot girth and he pounded into her as they built together for a climax. He tried to hold back, but the human in him was not around to take control. He grabbed a hold of his lover's hips and thrust into her, knowing that they were the perfect fit together. And even the beast did not want to let her go. He could feel that and knowing that both of his personalities yearned to be with Alika for all time, he thrust into her one last time and came with a loud roar while she howled.

She collapsed on top of him and then rolled to the side to nestle up to his side. She buried her head against his shoulder. Phillip was able to feel his humanity take over and let his shape switch back to human. And for the first time, it was not painful. The sluggishness of sleep wove through his muscles. He snuggled against Alika's chest, loving how her breasts cradled his head. "That was different."

"I told you it wouldn't be so bad if you just embraced it. You almost had it there for a few minutes. Next time it'll be different."

Phillip nodded and wondered whether he would ever be able to master the curse that gripped him.

* * * *

Phillip stared at the setting sun, and the change was weighing down his bones. He had wondered if he would be able to control it this time. Alika said it would not happen right away. He would have to get comfortable with this other side and stop thinking of it as a curse. But how could he do that when it had been that way for centuries? Maybe she was right, and he could overcome it and be one with it the same way she was with her wolf side. Alika still lay curled in the sleeping bag after their lovemaking. He was completely satisfied and knew that no matter what happened, he was going with her. She had talked about other women on her planet offering themselves to him, but he was not so sure about that. It was difficult to fathom that he was even going to leave the planet. If he did, would the curse leave him? He was not sure. Keeping a careful eye on the horizon, he saw something shoot across the sky. Her device began to beep.

Alika woke up and then grabbed her communicator. She pressed a few buttons and looked at him. "They're here! They made it."

"That's wonderful. When are they going to pick you up?"

She pressed her fingers to the side of her cheek. He heard a voice that sounded high-pitched and melodic, the same way Alika's did. She responded in her language, and he was not able to understand. It appeared that she was happy because she got up and bounced around the cave. He watched her for as long as he could and began stripping. It was time for Bigfoot to take over. The twists of agony always started in the pit of his stomach and spread like fire through his body. On instinct he tried to fight it. All his muscles tightened. Phillip fell to the floor, gripping his head. A scream came from his mouth, and he felt her hands on him.

"Shh…relax. Remember before, when we were togeth-er. How it felt. I'm with you. Don't let it plague you. Embrace the gift you were given."

He breathed, and some of the pain eased. The transfor-mation seemed to lift off of him. Phillip closed his eyes and still felt the burden of it. He saw his beloved's face in his mind. It was the first time he had seen it in so long. A wave of peace washed over him. His body relaxed. In Kaylana's eyes he saw love and peace. When that happened, he felt his body change. When he opened his eyes, he had completed the change and was still in Alika's arms. She hugged him strongly and then kissed him.

"See. Much easier."

He nodded.

She returned to the device and tapped in a few more numbers. "We need a place where the ship can land. Can you suggest something?"

Phillip saw the overhead images that flashed across the laptop screen. He pointed at one a couple of miles away with a flat space where they could land the ship. *"There's the best place, and we can get there quickly. When is it coming?"*

Alika asked this question, and her brow furrowed. "She said in a couple of hours. She has to circle around the moon first. She's been trying to avoid detection from any of the countries here. Do you think we should leave now?"

Phillip glanced at the sky, searching for some sign of the craft. *"We can. We just have to be careful and take everything that you need."*

Alika nodded and proceeded to take one of the backpacks, filling it with the things she needed, including the device she had rigged up and a couple of the loose crystals. She folded the clothes that Phillip had and added a few bottles of water. He had nothing else to take with him. All of his books were back at the other cave, and that had been ransacked.

"I think I have everything."

He nodded. Phillip felt a sense of remorse settle over him as he would never see the cave again, but he knew that was okay. It was time to make another life for himself. He took a light and led Alika through the cave system. They emerged into the night. Phillip sniffed the air, trying to smell any humans around, and he did not. He led Alika through the woods toward the landing site. Halfway there, he heard knocking, echoing in the distance, and some shrill whistles. He motioned for Alika to stop.

"What is it?"

"Bigfoot hunters."

"Hunters? Are they going to find you?"

Phillip heard the fear in her face. He chuckled. *"It's nothing you need to worry about. They are searching for evidence that I exist."* Plucking a few hairs from his pelt, he left them on a tree trunk. *"They are scientists and not harmful. Come on."* He slipped his fingers through hers and led her to the landing site.

The clacks and the howls continued, getting a little closer. He pressed his foot down into the soft earth so they could find a footprint. A flash of light appeared in the sky. Alika squeezed his hand. Her smile spread from ear to ear. Seeing the elation, he knew that this was what she had wanted all along. Phillip hugged her close. It was just a matter of time. A loud rumble started above them that shook the air and his bones. However, no wind stirred the trees or the air around him. He glanced up and saw no ship; all he saw was the reflection of the stars and the land. The craft had to be cloaked in some way.

"Hold it right there!"

They were surrounded by men dressed in black, pointing guns at him and Alika. Phillip snarled and shoved her behind him. Nothing was going to happen to her. The rumble of the craft above him did not faze the army as they advanced slowly. He growled and held her closer. There was nowhere for them to escape. The men with guns were on three sides, and the ship was at their back. All he needed was for it to open, and they would make a run for it. Hopefully,

Alika's comrade would have some defense system or weapon to protect them.

"I won't let them hurt you. No one is ever going to hurt you."

"They won't. We just have to keep them busy for a couple of minutes." Alika gripped his arm.

The men were closing in around them. As they did, the line before them parted and two men wearing lab coats stood before them. One had a clipboard. They were talking among themselves, and he did not like the subject of their conversation.

"You were right! She's green. I can't believe it! You won the bet. I wonder if she's from Orion." This was the younger of the scientists with blond hair and thick, black, rimmed glasses. He was shorter than the others by a good foot and somewhat round.

"Jeez, Cleveland. She's not an Orion slave girl from *Star Trek*." The other man shook his head and then flashed a smile at them. Phillip could smell their fear. It was a pungent odor that hung about them. He figured that they were trying to mask it with the small talk.

"Sorry, Mike, but damn. She's hot for an alien chick," Cleveland commented.

"Get over it. See what's standing next to her. I've always dreamed it was true. Bigfoot is real!" the other scientist said.

Of course I'm real, you idiots. Now stop being fucking nerds and let us get out of here. Phillip smiled at them. He raised his arms and stepped forward. The scientist shied away. He made a low grunt of frustration and the other men screamed like women. It was apparent that they assumed he was going to attack them. Phillip could not help but laugh. After a moment, Mike appeared to get up the courage to approach them. He held out a hand and slowly stepped toward Phillip.

"Nice, Bigfoot! We don't want to hurt you or your...er...friend."

Alika stepped out from behind Phillip. "If you didn't want to hurt us, then what is with the guns?"

"You can understand me?" the scientist asked. The guards raised their guns, but the scientist gestured for them to lower them. "Wait. Just wait."

"Of course I can understand you. I do have a translator that allows me to understand your base language. Don't you realize that we just want to leave this place?"

"But there is so much that we can learn from the both of you," Cleveland said.

Phillip stepped closer to Alika to protect her. *"Are you sure you want to talk to them?"*

She gave him a look that he figured meant to leave her alone and that she knew what she was doing. "You can learn whatever you want from my ship that you stole. But you're not getting me or Phillip."

"Bigfoot has a name?" the other man asked her.

Before she could answer, lights split the sky and the ship above them revealed itself. The blast from the engines blew many of the men backward and sent the scientists running. The door yawned open. Everyone froze. All they had to do was board the ship, and they could be gone. He would not miss the guns and waiting to be caught. All the hiding would be behind him. A woman much like Alika, wearing a black leather bodysuit, walked down the ramp. Alika ran toward the female coming toward them. At that moment, Phillip heard a shot. One of the soldiers must have gotten spooked and fired. It headed directly for Alika. He jumped in front of the bullet and felt the sudden heat hit him square in the chest. He fell back and landed on the bottom of the spaceship's ramp. He heard commotion around him and then the rumbling of the engines again. After that, there was nothing but blackness.

* * * *

Alika's face appeared above him. Her beautiful jade cheeks were streaked with tears. He reached up and brushed a stray one away. Phillip noticed that his hand was human and not hairy. "Why are you crying?"

The sadness in her eyes cracked when she realized that he was alive. "You were dead. You transformed back into a man, and you weren't breathing. We tried to heal you, but not even the machine could do anything."

He sat up slowly, drew her into his arms, and kissed her lightly on the lips before cupping her face in his hands. "You don't have to worry about me. I heal from all my wounds. It might take a while for me to come back, but I always do. Getting shot hurts though. Are you okay?"

"I'm fine. We dragged you into the ship and then took off. They shot at us, but it didn't damage the hull. We lifted off after that. We've just passed Saturn. It will take us a little while to get back to Rovan. Elarna's not pushing the ship. I hope this is what you wanted."

Phillip lifted Alika into his arms and held her close. This was all he desired. "It doesn't matter what planet or moon I'm on. The only thing I ever wanted was to be with you. I'll follow you across any solar system."

"Well, you won't have to chase me across the solar system. I'll always be here for you."

He kissed her, pressing his lips to hers. "I love you, Alika. My green beautiful alien."

She giggled. "And I love you, my gigantic hairy beast."

Phillip smiled and still felt the Bigfoot living inside of him. For the first time, he decided that he was not cursed at all. He was blessed. A woman loved him, and he was off to discover new adventures with her on another planet where wondrous things awaited him.

Come & Yeti

Chapter One

Swirling black clouds blanketed the sky, covering the three suns. The heavy gale compacted more snow against the five foot drift that partially hid the front of his dwelling. The colossal storm raged outside, and the howling wind reminded him of a wounded Griglach. It sent a few shivers under his fur. The drafts reached deep inside his cave and stirred the flames of his fire. The warmth was not something he needed; he used it for the light and to cook his food. Unlike others of his kind, he did not rely on technology to assist him. He didn't need a house made of stone, metal, and ice. Living in the mountains like his ancestors was what he was meant to do. No one understood his need to give in to his animal urges, the primal side of the Yetan nature to hunt with his claws and teeth. Others of his kind looked down upon him, but it didn't stop them from coming to him when they needed to be healed.

With the severity of the storm, he heard the Griglach hide flapping about. He sighed and picked up one of the luma stones he used to light the darker parts of the cave. The cavern had an abundance of the luma stones. The stone he chose was a foot long and three inches around. When he blew on it, the warmth of his breath interacted with the crystal, and it illuminated a light blue. He charged a few by the fire in case he needed them. As he walked toward the front of the cave, he tore a leg from the sorna he'd caught, a large winged creature that had wandered into one of his snares attracted by the meat he had left behind. This one had a five foot wingspan and more fat on it than usual. It was a lucky catch. Sorna mostly kept to the air unless they were breeding and it was mating season. They made their nests deep in the ice by clawing out a hole with their four inch talons and dangerously curved beaks. He had gotten a few pecks even through his thick pelt. He took another bite before setting the drumstick down and headed toward the cave entrance

The luma stone gave him enough light to see through the snow storm. The large hide had been wrenched free from most of the pegs that held it into the stone. He thrust the luma stone into the snow drift and held fast against the battering wind. Some Yetan were thought to have been blown away by the great gusts. Ancient tales told that spirts had ridden the wind and stolen away his people, but he wasn't afraid of archaic legends or the gusts. He lifted a hunk of ice and pounded the fasteners back into the stone. Some of the ice shaved off with each whack, but the repairs were easier than he expected. Working on the last pin, he heard a whistling sound overhead and then a large boom. Golden light exploded in the sky and streaked across the horizon. As he watched, another smaller flash broke off from the main one. In an instant, a sonic boom whooshed across the landscape, sending a wave of snow throttling toward him. He braced himself for the impact but didn't know what had crashed. The surge washed over him and weighed him down, but he was far enough away that it didn't bury him. With one good shake, he rid himself of the snow. He grabbed the luma stone and decided to investigate what had fallen from the heavens.

As he approached the crater, he noticed a silver ship protruding out of the mountain of snow it was immersed in. Parts of the hull and the insides were scattered across the frozen landscape. His father's warnings sounded in his mind about how, in the past, their species had been hunted by beings who had come down from the sky. He had not seen this other race, but he didn't doubt his father. Exposed wires and other sections of the craft sparked as he got closer. The way it landed made him think it ought to have cracked into more pieces. The scent of burnt ozone lingered in the air. He scrunched his nose at the stench of some putrid fluid that poured out of one side of the craft. Others from the village would be coming soon to investigate the crash. If they found any survivors they would be brought back to the town to be examined.

He should leave it alone, but he noticed a form submerged in the white drifts. An arm and a leg clad in black material was a stain upon the pristine snow. Off in the distance a loud shriek echoed on the wind. The storm had slowed, but it was only a lull. One look at the sky and the dark clouds told him that it would start up again soon.

When he looked up, he saw a two, large Gorap flying toward the crash site. Their black skin was slicked down with a few feathers. Their twenty foot wingspan made it easy for them to slice through the air. The Yetan Guard rode them for air patrols if any ship or foreign object came down onto the planet. They would take back anything they found and return to gather the remains of the vessel. He only had a few minutes before he would be spotted among the wreckage. He worked his way through the thigh high drifts and came upon a passenger that had been thrown from the spaceship. He scooped under the arm and leg and pulled out a female. He pressed his ear to her chest and barely heard her heart beating. As he listened, he realized there were two thumps instead of one. A small moan passed from her lips when he readjusted his hold on her and hugged her close. Once she touched his pelt, his whole body was electrified. It was his body's reaction to her internal injuries because he had the ability to heal. First he had to get her out of the frigid environment. With her thin skin she would not survive long in these harsh conditions. She coughed when he moved her and a green liquid he assumed was blood bubbled over her lips. She muttered something in a lyrical tongue that he could not understand.

"Don't worry," he answered her. "I'll make sure you're safe." He held her against his chest, knowing that she would be warm from his pelt. His body shook again as he fought the transformation that threatened to overtake him. He gritted his teeth, but he was in control. As he trudged through the snow, the Goraps' shrieks sounded above him once more. Snow fell harder than before, but it blanketed his footprints. The wind picked up again, slicing him with cold even through his fur. He breathed out and felt ice crystals forming around his mouth and nose. Standing out here was not doing any good. He used the luma stone's light to make his way back to the cave. Once he entered the hollow, he tugged on the hide to make sure it was secure once more. He rushed to the back and placed her on his bed of furs. He laid his hand on her forehead and a spike of agony speared his spine as he felt her internal injuries were worse than he realized. She didn't have long to live. When he pressed his head to her chest again, only one of her heats beat this time. He quickly stoked the fire and added a few lumps of coal to build up the heat. Thankfully, his cave was stone and not ice. He was far back within the mountains and if needed, he could navigate the tunnels that ran through them.

The fire grew higher. Condensation from the ceiling fell onto the flames and made them hiss. He glanced at the blaze to be sure it was still contained in the hearth. He turned his attention back to the woman. Her breathing was shallow. He was her only hope. Energy poured through him, and this time he didn't try to contain it. The change was coming upon him. He knelt before her and felt his form shrinking as he was able to take better stock of the woman before him. He grabbed a knife from the shelf above the bed carved into the wall. The black blade was made from a sorna's talon, and it was stronger than any metal weapon he owned. He slipped it through a hole in her garment and sliced it along her side and then over her chest so he could peel back the cloth. Once he had removed all her clothing and set it aside, then he could heal her. All the while, his form shrank and his hair receded. Once the transformation was complete, his hands were similar to hers except dark in color, almost as black as the female's clothing. He shook off the feeling of being hairless and focused on the woman before him. She had full breasts that were a darker indigo than her amethyst flesh. He closed his eyes, and in his mind's eye he saw the internal structure of the alien. One of her two hearts had been pierced by a couple of broken ribs. Some of her other organs that he didn't have a name for were also damaged. Her healing would take more than one session for him. All he had to do now was get her stabilized. Her remaining heart was creeping to a halt.

The heat of the fire seared his bare skin. Sweat beaded on his forehead that he wiped away with the back of his hand. Then he placed his hands on her chest. The intense wave of pain that consumed him made him cry out. He had worked on serious injuries before, but her physiology was different than what he was used to. His instincts guided him like a sixth sense so he could heal the woman. Underneath his discerning hands, the bones of her ribcage rearranged and clicked back into place. Once that happened, she inhaled a large breath, but she wasn't out of danger. More sweat ran down his brow as the heat ignited within him and settled over his heart. He concentrated the energy down his hands and into her slowing heart. After it hit the organ, it started beating at a normal pace once more.

With that done, he felt a little bit better. Now he could focus on her other heart. It had not restarted. It was dead in her chest. He knew that without the other beating she could not be able to live. More warmth, stronger than before, gathered within him. It seemed he would burn up from all of the energy. He ground his teeth as another bolt buzzed along his muscles. He screamed when he pushed that energy into the other heart located diagonally from the other one. It took a moment before it started. Once it did, he could feel the punctures in it healing. There was still more for him to do, but he just didn't have enough stamina to completely repair any more major injuries. Instead, he went through her system slowly and made sure he healed what he needed to do to keep her alive so he could recover his strength.

When she was no longer in danger, he let out a sigh of relief. Exhaustion had him. He took a deep breath and spread his hands before the fire to warm them. He flinched at his hairless flesh and thought how different his ebony skin was compared to his pure white pelt. Right now he couldn't muster the power to shift back into his rightful form. No matter how grateful others were when he healed them, his hairless appearance always brought ridicule. The blaze lulled him into a half sleep. He watched the flames dance and felt his eyes close.

The alien woman mumbled something, and it brought him out of his stupor. He turned back to her and touched her cheeks. She was hot. He scrunched his forehead together as he tried to figure out what he had missed. He placed his hands on the center of her chest once more and tried to sense what else was wrong, but there was nothing. Maybe she just burned hotter than his species. She babbled again and opened her eyes. Under those purple lids were the bluest eyes he had ever seen. They focused on him for a second before she closed them again. He waited to see if she would awaken once more, but she slipped deeper and deeper into slumber. He pulled a blanket over her half-naked form. He didn't need her dying from a chill after all the work he had done. The fire had burned down, and he could feel the nip in the air on his naked flesh.

He stood up, and his muscles took on greater mass from regaining his original form. His instincts said his charge would be okay for now and didn't require any more mending at the moment. He rolled his shoulders to loosen his muscles once he returned to his Yetan form. He made his way back to the front of the cave to check to see if others had come from the city to commandeer the ship's wreckage. He peeked through a hole in the Griglach hide and saw the Yetan Guard had set up a perimeter around the crash site. The red sashes they wore stood out against the white landscape. If the royal guard was involved, he prayed they would not come into his cave. Just in case, he would set aside some provisions and made sure he had a quick getaway planned. They would not get their hands on her. If that happened, there was no telling what experiments they would perform. He did not want to see her eviscerated and used for study. He remained still and observed as the guard collected what debris they could carry. Then he slipped back and snuffed out the fire lest they see the smoke escaping from behind the hide. He gathered a few more hides and piled them on top of the woman so she could stay warm.

He gathered some dried sorna jerky, a few pieces of clothing for her and for him if he changed back into his hairless shape. Then he slipped under the furs with the alien and molded his body to hers, covering her the best he could so the extra blankets, hides, and his furs could keep her warm. Already she was trembling and the temperature was plummeting. Even with the fire extinguished, the luma stones embedded in the cave wall gave off a faint blue light, enough that he could see her. She was peculiar and attractive wrapped into one fine package. Her hair was shoulder length and white as his pelt. Her eyelashes and eyebrows were the same hue as her hair. Her cheekbones were sharp like the fine edge of a luma crystal. She wasn't beautiful in the way he was used to because all Yetan females were covered in hair.

She was unique.

His guest whispered something once more in her lyrical tongue and thrashed around. He laid his hand on her forehead. "Don't worry. You're safe. No one is going to harm you while you're with me. I swear."

Chapter Two

Phillip opened his eyes slowly. Everything hurt. The last thing that he remembered was the sudden barrage of the alarms sounding off in the spaceship he was on with Alika. They had only been on it a few days since they had left Earth and were heading back to her planet. The distress signal she had set off had been picked up by her friend, Elarna, who had rescued them. There they were supposed to live a happy life. However, that had all changed when the ship's warning system had broadcasted around them.

He tried to sit up, but a sharp stab traveled up his shoulder. He closed his eyes and took in a deep breath against the pain, knowing that he would heal. One thing about his condition he appreciated was that he mended no matter what the damage done to him. Whatever his injuries were, he had to find Alika. The last time he had seen her was when she shoved him into some kind of escape pod so that he would be safe. Phillip had tried to argue with her, but she wouldn't listen and thrust him into the pod. The metal door had come down over him. All he could do was pound on the glass and watch her lovely emerald face grow smaller and smaller as he moved away from the falling ship. The crash had knocked the wind out of him. When he opened his eyes, he realized the escape pod had shattered around him into tiny pieces. One of those fragments had embedded into his shoulder. He gripped the metal shard and pulled it from his flesh. Once it was out, it immediately felt better. Phillip threw it away from him and got up slowly.

He took in the alien planet he had crash landed onto. Gazing around, he understood what it had been like for Alika when she had hurtled down to Earth, onto a foreign world. He was in the same position, staring at the white wasteland around him. The atmosphere felt heavier than what he was used to and so did his body, but he could breathe with ease, so at least the planet wasn't devoid of oxygen. Phillip glanced up at the sky. Violet tinged, gray clouds showered white flakes down upon him that he assumed was snow. It inundated the landscape so it was impossible to see more than a few feet in front of him. Phillip held out his hand and caught a few snowflakes on his fingers. Against his brown fur it dissolved a little slower. He flicked his tongue over the melted snow. It tasted like the snow back home with a slightly salty aftertaste. The wind whipped around him, stirring his pelt. The glacial atmosphere tried to break through his large frame and blow him over. At least his cursed form as a Bigfoot came in handy and kept him warm. On Earth he hated being what he was, but maybe here it was a boon.

Phillip wiggled his toes in the snow and felt like he was on solid ground. With the snow coming down fast, he figured he had to get out of the open. If this planet was inhabited, then someone would come to investigate what had landed. He did not want to be there and become the subject of some science experiment. Also there was no way to tell what kind of wildlife was on the planet either. There might be nothing more than a stray bird or some alien version of a goat, but there could also be predators. He could handle whatever came at him on Earth, but here was a different story. At home he could tap into the elements, and they assisted him in finding shelter, food, or other things. Sometimes they were his only companions during his long existence. Maybe he could tap into the elements on this world too. He closed his eyes and reached out his senses to feel the wind. The angry tempest howled around him and didn't want to help him. He pushed his awareness down, below all the layers of ice and snow to the ground. Once he touched up its energy, it seemed glad to aid him because it had been neglected.

He took in a deep breath and moved deeper down. He didn't sense any plant life. *Is this place mostly covered in ice and snow? Does it ever get green?* On Earth he had traveled into Canada toward the North Pole, but even among the polar bears and the reindeer it was too barren and bleak for him. Phillip didn't enjoy the cold and preferred the deep forests and mountains where he had many places to hide just in case someone came looking for him. Although, he didn't have to worry about leaving any signs of his presence unless he wanted to. On this planet, he hoped the same principles applied.

Phillip felt the rock below all the ice. It was mostly the same as it was back on his world. He asked it to show him to the nearest shelter and where there had been a disturbance somewhere on the planet if it was close. It took a moment, but the energy of the rocks rose to the surface and settled into his bones so he felt connected with the element. It was a magnetic force that rolled through his body, and he knew it would show him the way. He focused first on searching for any place where the main craft had landed, but after scouring the countryside there wasn't anything except rising snow mounds. He ran through the snow, but in some places the drifts came up to his chest, making the trek arduous. His coat kept him warm. When he looked back to see if he had a trail behind him, the snow had collapsed around the path he had plowed through, and it had already filled in his footprints. No matter how hard and far he looked, he couldn't find the wreckage of the main ship. As he trudged through the blizzard, Phillip found breathing was laborious. The air was thicker than what he was used to, but he muddled through it until he came to an ice-covered waterfall.

The snow stopped for an instant, and a ray of sun slipped between the clouds. Within the silence of the storm, Phillip glanced up and saw three large suns. One was purple. Another was orange, and the third was yellow like the one he was used to. It was also the closest. A shaft hit the waterfall. Rainbows burst over the snow, refracting through the ice. Behind the frozen water he glimpsed a slim opening. He squeezed through the narrow aperture. He inhaled the air within the cave and didn't find it stale or having the scent of an animal in it. Instead it was dry inside, and when he breathed in again he caught the faint aroma of something burning. It wasn't wood or coal. It was something different. He sniffed again and realized it was bone. The raw material was difficult to burn, and had a distinctive smell that coal didn't, but it kept the fire blazing hotter. He would burn any other large animal bones if he found them before he had pilfered lighter fluid from the campers he stumbled upon.

Phillip moved deeper into the cave system. He had assumed it would be covered with moss or strange creatures ready to attack him, but there was nothing in the cavern so far that didn't remind him of home. While on his journey with Alika, she had told him about her home planet, Rovan. It was more jungle than Earth. There were countless valleys where great herds of animals roamed and were untouched by civilization because it was forbidden. Some parts of the planet were only night and the other parts were day. And at certain points the night and the day shined as one, it just depended on where one stepped. He longed to see the plants and the skies of her world and the green pools she talked about. The only thing he wasn't so keen about was that men were scarce so women shared their mates. Phillip wanted to keep her to himself, but first he had to find her.

He inhaled the scent of the burning bone and stopped at a junction too narrow for him in his current seven foot five inch tall frame. In his human form, he was six feet and four inches tall, but in his current guise it was nearly impossible for him to push through some of the places within the cave. He willed himself into human form and gritted his teeth when the beast inside of him fought to take back control. He ducked through the tight space. Rock scraped against his flesh and caused him to hiss from the sudden pain. He trudged forward until he came to a place that forked five different ways. Three of the tunnels had old air coming from them. The other two both had fresh air, so he couldn't tell where the smoke originated from. Mixed with the aroma of the smoke, he smelled a predator. It had the same gamey scent of a beast, similar to a bear, and yet there was something deeper to it he couldn't quite place. He turned to head to the other cave that he could venture down, but the fragrance of smoke was lighter. Something tugged on his insides and told him this was the way to go. If the predator turned out to be some kind outer space polar bear he would deal with it. Besides, he had claws of his own that could slice and dice anything that came after him.

He moved slowly through the cave as it led further into the earth. It grew a little warmer as he descended. The crystals in the walls glowed faintly blue, giving him the light to see by. He got to one flooded passage, but the scent of the hunter was stronger than it had been before. He slid into the water and expected it to be frigid, but it was tepid. There had to be a thermal shaft or geothermal spot within the cavern that brought the heat into this part of the cave. He didn't sense any life within the pool, so he walked until the water was up to his waist. When he lost his footing his head dunked underneath the water. He broke the surface and spit out the water he had swallowed, tasting a bit of sulfur. Phillip kept swimming while searching for more light, but it was all black. His senses drove him forward until he smacked his head on the ceiling of the cave. He had to crawl through the passageway to get to the other side. Once he inhaled, he caught the scent of smoke mingled with the predator. It was a stronger smell of musk rolled in cloves.

The hair stood up on his body as he approached a passageway that led into a bigger room. He moved slowly, keeping his claws ready in case something came at him. Phillip listened, heard nothing, so he crept forward. The cavern opened up into another room. This one reminded him of the cave he had called home on Earth. He saw another opening and instead of it being open there was a covering across it. Someone lived here. Phillip crept toward the hide, hoping that his approach was silent. The earth element grounded and guided him as he had asked, but he released it then so he could focus on the things he would find on the other side of the drape.

Phillip pulled it back and glanced around, realizing he had stepped into the sleeping chambers of the cavern's inhabitant. The walls were lined with the glowing blue crystals. He saw the remnants of a fire pit. He didn't see anything in the way of technology at least that he was used to, a radio, a flashlight, or even anything metallic. Maybe this civilization was primitive and had not figured out how to fashion such things. This was where the aroma of the bones and the beast originated from. A large shape huddled underneath some hides in the corner across from the hearth. He stepped into the room, not wanting to wake whoever was sleeping. As he studied the mound, he noticed a few strands of white hair. He breathed in again and caught the metallic scent of blood. It had been cloaked by the fire. In the corner was a heap of black clothing. The person beneath the blankets was Elarna. She had rescued them from Earth and from the military that was after him and Alika.

Now here she was being cared for by someone. Maybe Alika was with them. He didn't see her green form, but maybe she was also below all those furs. *Please be okay.* He went over to her, knelt down, and peeled back the layers of pelts on top of her.

Elarna was sleeping. Scratches adorned her face and ran down her neck. They hadn't been there the night before and looked already healed. She must have been wounded in the crash, but how badly was she wounded? Before Phillip could rouse her, a great whoosh of air surrounded him and then he was slammed into the wall. It took a moment for the stars to fall from his vision. Before him was a beast at least eight feet tall. It was completely white with large hands and bigger feet than him. He had an elongated snout, but he reminded Phillip of all the descriptions he had seen or heard about the abominable snowman. Phillip was aware that people called him a Yeti at times even though he was a Bigfoot. This creature was something he expected to see in the deep mountain valleys of Nepal where snow and ice covered the landscape most of the year. He had searched Earth for something that resembled him. Once he had come across a trace of another Bigfoot, but he had never met one. Here on a distance planet he had stumbled across a true Yeti.

A space Yeti at that.

The Yeti roared something, but Phillip didn't understand him. He stood up slowly, hoping the creature would understand he was not a threat. He took a step toward Elarna, but the beast jumped in front of him, blocking her. Phillip wanted to say something, but all that came out was a grunt mixed with a short howl. Alika had implanted a translator into the center of his forehead so that they could understand one another. When he was in his beast form she read his thoughts. Even when she was in her second form as a large wolf, she could talk to him telepathically. He wasn't sure if that was the case with this behemoth before him. Hell, he didn't even know really how the translator worked or how to adjust it.

Can you understand me? Phillip thought at the creature. He waited to see if the other understood him.

The yeti cocked his head, but it didn't seem that he did. Phillip sighed and searched round for something that might help him to get his point come across. He spied some kind of knife. When he reached for it, the other beast swatted at him and growled. Phillip bowed his head and held up his hands showing he submitted his dominance to the creature. He glanced up and saw the beast studying him. Phillip moved slowly and took the knife. The yeti seemed to be waiting for him to see what he was doing. He realized the yeti must have visited the crash site in order to bring Elarna back. He scratched a rough picture of the ship, a saucer shape coming down from the atmosphere and then breaking apart. He drew the smaller pod that he was in and then two shapes near the bigger ship. He pointed at Elarna, himself and then back at the ship, hoping the beast would get the idea. The yeti studied him for a while and then gestured at himself and Elarna.

Phillip nodded, but he needed to know if this creature had seen Alika. He pointed at the second figure by the ship. The yeti shook his head and motioned to Elarna once more. He hung his head and sighed. Phillip slammed his hand down into the dirt. Pain shot up his arm as he realized he had broken something. It would dissipate when his body repaired itself. A jolt of energy raced along his arm. He looked up and no longer looked to the hairy face of the creature. Instead, he saw a dark skinned man with deep green eyes. His hair was as white as the snow outside. Phillip tried to pull his hand away, but he couldn't.

"I can heal your wounds," the man before him said.

Phillip understood him now that he was in a human or humanoid form. He nodded and took a deep breath and tried to push the Bigfoot back within his mind away. It took him a couple of moments before he had shrunk down into his man form as well.

The yeti's eyes widened. "How did you do that?"

Phillip hoped he could maintain his human form. "Thank you for trying to heal me, but you don't have to worry about it. My body will restore itself. Can you understand me?"

"In this form yes, I can understand you. Please, how did you do that?"

"It's complicated. Did you find another woman with Elarna?"

"No. As I tried to tell you before, there was only her. This other woman, she is like this one?"

"She is my..." Phillip didn't think wife was an appropriate word for Alika nor was she his girlfriend. "Mate." He ended up saying. That seemed to be the best description of their relationship.

The other nodded in comprehension. "Mate. Yes, I understand this. I did not see her, only this female in the wreckage of the great ship that fell from the sky. I searched the remains where it had broken up, but most of it was buried in the snow. I barely recovered her. Then the royal guard arrived and surrounded the ship. They'll go through it and bring any survivors back to the compound. How do you do this, change your form? I thought I was the only one."

"We have to the go and find Alika. We have to go and..."

The other held up his hands. "No. We can't. There's nothing we can do. The whole city will know you're not one of us. They will know you have come from the craft. Besides, I can't leave her. She still has injuries that I haven't healed completely. Her wounds were grievous, and it took much of my energy to repair them."

It sounded like the other male was a healer, but he still wasn't sure. Phillip gritted his teeth at the beast, pushing back against the human half. He had to keep the Bigfoot at bay for a while longer. The anger from not being able to find Alika weighed on him. He ran his fingers through his hair. She could be out in the elements, freezing to death. She could be at the mercy of the royal guard, or worse she could be dead. Phillip refused to believe that she was dead. He had to find her and this...man was his only link to her. "What's your name? Where am I? Where did we smash onto?"

"My name is Heragthan," the yeti replied.

Phillip heard the name, but it sounded as though the other man had swallowed half of it. He didn't think he could pronounce most of it. "Hergman." He articulated carefully.

The other man frowned.

"Herrrman," he tried again.

The other seemed to accept that. He touched his chest. "Phillip." Then he pointed at the woman on the bed. "Her name is Elarna."

Herman nodded and said the name to himself very low, but it was enough that Phillip heard it. The beast within wanted back out, but he held it at bay for a little longer, remembering what Alika had told him about trying to be in sync with it. He needed more time to talk with Herman. He smiled when he thought about Herman, the Space Yeti. There would be a story to tell in this. Of course he still had to find Alika first and get off the planet. No one was going to hurt his mate.

"Phhiilllipp." Herman strung the sounds together, but he did better than Alika had the first time she had said his name. "Yes. How is it that I can understand you in this form when I couldn't in the other?"

Phillip tapped the center of his forehead. "Alika implanted a universal translator in the center of my head so

I can understand her and I guess you, but it doesn't work when I'm in my Bigfoot form. Only then I can hear her thoughts. I guess it allows me to understand you and vice versa. But I won't be able to understand you while you're a yeti."

"Y-yet-ti? What is that?" Herman asked.

"Where I'm from, there are stories of beasts that resemble your other form; tall, white hairy monsters that live in the snow up in the mountains. Sometimes humans find large footprints and make copies of them to show the rest of the world. They even do that with me. They call me Bigfoot because of my large feet, but I've never come across anyone else like me."

"I have not heard of these h-h-uma-nns. But they are like your other form?"

"No. They look like me as I am now. This is how I was before I was cursed. Beast by night and man by day. Live for all eternity no matter what happens to me. What about you?"

"My people. We are beasts...." Herman screwed up his face as though he was in pain. He backed away and his dark skin was covered once again by a thick white pelt. He stood up, towering above Phillip.

It was then he felt his own body shifting back into the Bigfoot. There was no need to fight it. If Alika was with him, she would have been able to keep him from changing back. But she was not. He had to find her. He knew now that he couldn't do that without Herman's help. He prayed that Elarna would awaken soon so he could ask her what happened and why they had crash landed. Maybe those answers would assist him. Maybe she knew if Alika had gone to another life pod or been at the helm too. Phillip dismissed the notion that she was buried somewhere under the ice. He couldn't fathom the idea of never being able to look upon her stunning emerald face ever again.

Chapter Three

Elarna opened her eyes. It took a moment for her to realize she was lying down and staring up at a stone ceiling. Blue crystals embedded in the walls and the ceiling illuminated the space so she could see. Every muscle in her body cried out in pain. When the ship had been going down, she didn't have time to make it to the escape pod. The alarm had sounded, tugging her from sleep because the craft was on autopilot speeding them back to Rovan. Her flight path had kept her clear of space debris, asteroid belts, and far enough away from enemy planets they shouldn't have had to worry about anything. However, something had gone wrong. She had sprinted to the controls and....

The rest was blank from there no matter how much she tried to search her memory for it.

Must have gotten a bad bump on the head. Thank the goddess Geru I'm alive. As she sat up, her side pained her. She placed her hand over her left side, and it seemed that one of her ribs was out of place. When she tried to turn over on her good side, her leg screamed in agony and she fell back onto the bed. Right now she wished for the healing bed in her ship or to be back on Rovan where the healers could touch a person and mend any injury someone had. *So much for trying to get up and figure out where in the universe I am.* Elarna took in more of her surroundings from her limited viewpoint. A fire pit with a small fire popped a few feet from her, throwing off warmth into the room. The air was cool around her exposed limbs. She examined the blankets and noticed some were hides from some large animals and some were woven fabric. She ran her hand over them and felt a mixture of fur and scales.

She heard a grunt and saw something large move in the room. A twinge of fear gripped her as many possibilities of what it could be went through her mind. If she was going to have been eaten, she would be dead already. Being in an unfamiliar place and unfamiliar surroundings, the trepidation of her situation caused her two hearts to beat rapidly. She drew in another breath and tried to stay calm. It could be many things that this shadow could belong to. It could, in the end, just be a shadow. However, the silhouette gave way to a large, apelike creature. At first she thought it was a *gorenaut*, a giant gray primate that lived in the forests on her planet. They were eight feet tall and weighed between six hundred and eight hundred pounds. They were vicious beasts that even weathered hunters avoided. Her brother had once tried to go after one and never returned. Her brother had been such a prize with beautiful lavender skin and white hair. Sharim already had three brides lined up, but he didn't listen and went to prove himself against the gorenaut.

Now one stood before her. She froze.

As a child they were warned that if ever confronted by a gorenaut, she should freeze. Don't look it in the eye. The primates were the largest predator on the planet besides the *lolliz*, an enormous six legged, nine hundred poud serpent that lived in the wastelands. One bite could kill besides spitting poison onto its prey. Some tried to tame them to ride because they were fast, but not many were successful to tell the tale.

The beast moved into the room. From her position all she could see were its large seven toed feet. They were bigger than Alika's new mate's. They were covered in white fur, and the nails on the seven toes were curved long enough into claws so they could grip whatever the beast was walking on.

It knelt down next to her. She expected the worst, but it did nothing. Once she realized that, she mustered enough courage to look up and inspect the beast for herself. Instead of the gorenaut this creature's face was a mixture of ape and canine features where his muzzle was rounded like the primate, but slightly elongated with sharp teeth. Yet it was also very humanoid too. He reached toward her, but she shied away from him. An annoyed look crossed his features, and he let out a long snort. He said something, but it came out more as grunts and growls.

Elarna sighed and touched the left side of her face. Instead of feeling the small buttons that controlled the universal translator implanted along the side of her left cheek, she felt half of it. *Broken. Just my luck.* She shook her head. He held out his hands as though trying to tell her to wait. Before her eyes his large form shrunk down and all the hair receded from his body, leaving a male that resembled a human like Phillip. Instead, this man retained his seven toes and had a longer face. When he smiled his teeth were all sharp points.

"You have nothing to fear from me."

Her eyes widened. "I can understand you. Thank the goddess. I thought my translator was broken." A sense of some relief flooded her. "Are you the one who brought me here?"

He nodded. "I am. You were badly hurt in the crash. I …arhgou...outis."

She frowned as his words were swallowed up into a void of static. She held up her hand to get him to stop for a second. Elarna tapped her left temple, hoping the translator would work. It was probably loose wiring. If she had hit her head it made sense that something would have been jarred loose.

"Say something again," she requested.

"Origh trinata…"

She gritted her teeth and smacked the center of her forehead where the main module of the translator was located. The jarring pain hurt, but...

"I was saying that you were badly injured."

"Oh good."

"That you were hurt?" His eyebrows furrowed, but his green eyes were filled with concern.

"Huh-no. That's a bad thing. I assume I wasn't hurt very badly, or you wouldn't have been able to get me away from the ship."

"On the contrary, you were almost dead. It took a great deal of my energy to restart your heart and make sure your wounds were sealed so that you would survive the night. Your physiology is so different from mine in so many ways that it burned my normal amount of energy I would use when healing others of my kind."

Elarna nodded. It sounded reasonable. If he had healed her then that would make sense why he hovered, and yet there was something familiar in his other form besides looking like a gorenaut. "Where am I? Do you know what happened to the other passengers of my ship?"

"Hush. All of your questions will be answered later when you're better. For now, let me heal you. Lay back please."

She hated being given orders. Because of her stubbornness she had lost many things and gained others. Alika had stood by her when she had broken from her family tradition and became a procurer the way that Alika had. They went out looking for matable men. She had a grand time traveling the galaxy and finding herself in places she never been before. But when she had been called home because her mother was dying, she had been told she needed to take up once more with the family business and give up her ship. She had until her birthday to make that happen. When Alika never showed up and then the distress call came in, there was nothing or no one that could keep her from helping her friend. Now she had no idea where her friend was or what had happened to Phillip. Alika had shoved him into one of the escape pods. After that it was still all a blur.

The man before her laid a hand on her forehead and tried to pull down the blankets that covered her chest. She grabbed the furs and wouldn't release them. She was not about to let this male see her naked.

He chuckled. "I had to remove your clothing so I could heal you. I have already seen your womanly mounds. I won't harm you. Trust me."

Womanly mounds?

He waited patiently. He did seem to be telling her the truth. Finally, she relented and released the covers. He placed another hand on her chest. Once his palm settled on her skin a great heat flushed her body until sweat slid down her face. The pain eased, and something else happened. His energy filled her and made her tingle in every way possible. This stranger wasn't touching her in a sexual way, but by the goddess if he didn't make her gush with desire for him. Her nipples hardened at the thought of him. From her perspective he was completely naked with nothing covering his genitals. His cock was semi-erect and rested against his thigh. Even in that state it was ten inches long. She felt her hearts skip a beat, picturing how he would be in bed and how he would be in his beast form. Elarna had always loved big, hairy males who could make her howl. In his other form, knowing he was not a threat, she could see herself mounting and riding him until he made her come, screaming.

He moved his hand from her chest, and it brushed her pert nipple, shooting desire through her. A small moan spilled from her lips.

"I apologize if this hurts," he said to her in a flat tone.

He leaned over and pressed his lips to the center of her chest where his right hand had been while he trailed it lower over her abdomen. He stopped at her navel and more warmth flooded her system as something within her moved back into place. It made her jump, but she was more focused on trying not to get lost in the pleasure that inundated her system. He was trying to heal her, and she was so turned on that it was embarrassing. It had been a long time since she had been with a male of any species.

"It doesn't hurt," she forced out. He trailed his tongue down the center of her chest, slightly scraping her flesh as it went. "What are you doing?" she asked, trying to keep her voice even.

"It helps me detect if there are any places that I missed or if there are toxins in your skin. They center around the heart. Since you have two, I wanted to be doubly sure that you have nothing else in your system. Most of your wounds are healed, so there'll only be one more time that I need to do this, and you'll be well again. It will take me some time to regain my strength. It takes more energy to heal you than what I'm accustomed to." He sat up and the creases in his forehead deepened. "Have I done something to offend or hurt you?"

"No. It's just…never mind." Elarna couldn't help but let her gaze trail down his chiseled physique and notice the etching of his muscles and how they stood out underneath his skin. He might have been all beast in one guise, but in this one he was all male. She tried not to want to feel this longing that had sprung up inside of her.

"Tell me," he insisted.

Elarna leaned over and planted her lips on his. He stiffened but did not pull away from her. She took his face between her hands and held him there. His skin was silky against her palms. When he responded, he kissed her lightly and then disengaged from her very slowly. He smiled.

"I-I'm s-sorry," she stammered as she realized what she had done. "I shouldn't have done that."

He trailed a finger down her cheek. "There's no need for apologetic. It happens quite often when I heal people."

"I think you mean apologies. Your patients always kiss you after you treat them?"

"They have this intense feeling that can arouse them. When a healer heals, it creates a bond between patient and healer. It's a normal reaction. Even the smallest wound with the exchange of energy it makes for a forged link. With your strange anatomy, I can't say how powerful the effects will be."

"Oh." She smiled and settled back down into the bed. Questions bounced through her mind. "Still. I'm sorry. I shouldn't have forced myself upon you with you being such a gracious host. But can I ask you a few more questions?"

He nodded, but before he could answer, Elarna heard heavy footsteps. She glanced over and saw a large, hairy, brown beast who trotted over to see her. She held out her hand. He took it in his and squeezed.

"You're okay," she said.

He nodded. He said something, but she couldn't understand him. "Sorry. My translator is broken."

He nodded again and she knew he understood what that meant. It took him a moment before he became human once more, but it seemed he struggled to keep the shape. Elarna found him to be more appealing when he was in his Bigfoot form and not in his human one. However, she wasn't going to argue because at least this way she could speak to him. She hoped he could fill in some of the holes that were in her memory.

"Are you okay?" Phillip asked.

"I am thanks to our host." She glanced at him and felt her cheeks burn, thinking about the kiss they had shared. It would be nice to get him alone so she could thank him for rescuing her.

"He has been very gracious and honestly this is just so very strange."

"Of course it is, you never thought of traveling beyond your planet. Humans have only just started exploring the galaxy, but it will be years before they get out of their solar system. Sorry, I'm not trying to put down your race, but you're very primitive, and there's a reason why we don't stop on your planet for potential mates. Can you tell me something about what happened?"

He curled his hand into a fist and squeezed his eyes shut as though he fought the shift back into his beast form. All the while her inner feline paced back and forth ready to pounce and romp across the planet until she found Alika. Then she would figure out a way to get off this rock. Phillip shook his head. "I don't really know. I woke up, and the alarm was going off. Alika ran to the cockpit to see what was going on. She was busy pressing some buttons and talking to the computer. You were screaming at it, but I don't know what you were saying; you were both going too quick; the translator wasn't catching everything."

She hung her head. They had planned to replace the broken one that Alika had implanted inside of Phillip's head with a newer version, but they hadn't gotten around to it. The voyage was supposed to be uneventful. When she had gone to sleep, they had two days before they arrived back at Rovan. She remembered a little bit more of what Phillip had told her. She recalled being at the navigation screen with the alarm sounding and the view screen had pulled up. Something had gotten in her way. Something that wasn't supposed to be there that hadn't been there on the way to Earth, but on the way back something had gone wrong. She couldn't remember exactly what. It was still a bit blank.

"I remember the computer warning that we were on a collision course. I couldn't stop it. No matter how much we tried. Alika…" She tried to recall more but couldn't.

Elarna felt a hand on her shoulder. When she looked over, Phillip had smiled at her. "It's okay. We have to find her. That's the most important thing. Then we have to leave this ball of ice they call a world. Of course I have no idea how we're going to do that."

Ball of ice. Did I hear him right? If that was true, then they were on a planet they weren't supposed to be on. It was forbidden. Kraztarn. The world was exactly what Phillip had said, a big sphere of ice with nothing except large hairy primates. They had procured some mates from Kraztarn years ago before they had started fighting back. She didn't want to think about the idea that Alika had been captured and was being dissected by the apes. And one of them had rescued her. Although she had never heard of them shifting into another form. From what she knew they were only single formed like humans, but Phillip was an exception.

"This place is all ice. Did this translate correctly?"

He nodded. "Yes. Everywhere I looked it was frozen. The driving blizzard wasn't letting up. I was lucky the earth elements here are similar to those on Earth. Some of the elements here didn't want to cooperate. The element led me into a cave. I followed it deeper and found the system that led me to Herman."

The skin rippled on his body, and he squeezed his eyes shut. It appeared he was fighting the transformation. He had explained to her that by day he was a man and by night he was a Bigfoot, but he retained his human intelligence. She had found it interesting there was something of a bit of magic on Earth because she had thought it was something that had died out eons ago. At least that was the story told on Rovan about earthlings. Humans were technologically slow. They were advancing, but they had lost touch with their elemental side. They had magic on Rovan through the goddess they worshipped and also embraced technology. Their major problem was their declining male population. Elarna had prayed to the goddess she would find a male who would love her, but she had never been so lucky. That was one reason they went off world to find mates. It didn't matter what species they were because most males were able to reproduce with Rovian women. She had never met any children who had not inherited the ability to take on the Rovian beast form of their dual nature. It just depended on what part of the planet one grew up on that made one into a certain kind of shifter.

Elarna was from the south where they were more trees, and her dual form was a large feline. Alika was from the west continent with open plains. Her tribe had inherited more of the canis trait, what Phillip called wolves. Once she had rescued them, Elarna had learned more about Phillip. She found him interesting and learning how he was transformed into the beast was heartwrenching. It had called to her. He had fallen in love with a woman, and the father didn't approve. Even being on the ship in his beast form, she couldn't help the attraction she felt for him. However, Elarna didn't want to approach Alika about the possibility of sharing her new mate. And she wasn't sure that the big hairy man would want to share with her or any other women.

It was tradition on their planet that one male would service eight to ten females. It might be that he had one or two specific mates that he spent time with, but because men were in such high demand, they were expected to divide their attention. Not too many women went out to procure males from other planets. There was the danger of ships crashing or getting caught by the inhabitants of the worlds they went to. Another scientific avenue was that they were searching for a genetic solution as to what was wrong with their population. Some Rovians blamed the heavy gravity of the planet to the amount of rain. Others accused the gods and begged them for help. Elarna wanted to be of service to fellow Rovians. After thirty successful missions, they were able to choose a male. Sometimes this took years. It was a tough mission and more worlds were becoming off limits because of their technological advances, disease, or some other reason. On one world she traveled to, the males were insectoid. Many of the females desired males with hair on them.

That was one reason that the ice planet was targeted for a couple of hundred years. It wasn't like they were taking numerous amounts of males off the planet. They took two or three at a time, and the rule was to always ask them. Rules stipulated that they only took unattached males. They weren't taken against their will. She understood how other cultures would think they were kidnapping their men. Kraztarn was deemed not accessible because several of the procurers had made it back barely alive with tales the Yetan started killing some or catching them for experimentation. Now there was an edict not to go to the planet.

She had allowed Alika to be taken. They were going to do horrible things to her. She thought about Phillip and knew he was worried about her. When Elarna looked up the wolf animal from Earth it had some similarities to Alika's canis form. Rovian legends about their dual forms was that the goddess gave the power of the animals to all walk upright on two legs, but they still had to fit into their respective environments. Others that said it all came down to two species cross-mating. She didn't care about any of it; Elarna just wanted a male in her life so she'd stop feeling so lonely. There was only so far that she could take a pleasure device.

Yeah, it was great for getting her off, but no matter how many appendages, tentacles, or vibrating brushes it had, it wasn't the same thing as a good old fashioned male prick.

When she thought about Phillip, all the hair got her going. Even in his human appearance there was some heat between them, but she hadn't wanted to take it up with Alika because they were still cementing their relationship. And she wasn't sure if he was ready to eventually take on another female. He wanted to stay with Alika. Apparently, on Earth, they did not take multiple mates.

Whenever a species was brought to Rovan they were categorized, blood was taken, and they were assigned women over time. Elarna had been with other females before. She and Alika had gone on long distance journeys and with nothing to do in space at times they engaged in sexual acts. Her friend was attractive and again served a basic need. She didn't mind being with a female, but it was all about the males. Something about how they smelled made her all gooey inside. Between Phillip being on the ship and her waking up in the cave permeated with the heady scent of the Yetan made her dizzy. Then he had touched her. It didn't matter if he was learning more about her anatomy. It had kicked her libido into high gear.

All she wanted to do was take him on the floor and feel his cock inside of her. She wanted him hairless or with hair. It didn't matter until she was riding him. She was wet just thinking about him. Hair, tall, and running his claws down her back while his dick filled her. Elarna had fucked some males who were scaled, some with feathers, others with barbs, just so long as she was fulfilled. Phillip moaned in agony as his features shifted. His nose and mouth had lengthened a bit and his forehead had grown larger. A fine layer of brown hair had sprouted on his skin.

"Don't worry, Phillip. Just let go. I can talk to Herr…man," she pronounced out the Yetan's name, but it didn't sound right on her tongue. There seemed to be a syllable or two missing, but with Phillip's translator malfunctioning he might have missed part of the name.

He nodded. Phillip's other form came through. His grew until he was over seven feet tall. His hands were clawed, and he was covered in matted, brown fur. He definitely was more attractive when he was hairy. Something about those claws and his feet. It was strange he had five toes though. All Rovians had six. How could he keep his balance with just five toes? He flashed her a grin, showing her his long, curved canines. His muzzle wasn't as pronounced now that he had fully transformed. She compared him to her host and realized the Yetan's muzzle was more oblong and pointed.

Phillip left the space, and her caretaker came back in. He carried something in his hands that smelled like meat and made her mouth water. Herman handed her a bone plate and made the motion that she should eat. She nodded. Elarna ripped the meat from the bone with a tug. The game was cooked and had a salty flavor, but she could taste the blood within it that made her inner cat emerge. It moved underneath her skin as she swallowed. She took another bite and felt her nails elongating into claws. The heady smell of Herman enticed the animal in her more. If her feline came out, there was no telling what would happen. She closed her eyes and breathed in. It was never this arduous to keep the cat under her skin. She was the one who controlled it and not the other way around. However, the need to mount this male drove the beast. Maybe it was because he said they were connected.

"What is it?" her host asked.

She opened her eyes and saw he was a beast no longer. "Why are you like that? I thought you could only be that way when you needed to heal someone?" Elarna forced out.

"True, but I just chose not to because of all of the things that it implies. I felt your pain so it triggered me to switch my forms. What's going on?"

She shook her head. *How can I tell him about how I'm feeling and the only thing that will stop it is being with him? How will he react when I shift?* This great need for a sexual release was not something she had experienced before. His influence over her was stronger than it appeared.

"You don't want to know. I need you to..." She arched her back as the vertebrae in her neck popped. Elarna lunged forward, going down on all fours. The plate of meat clattered to the ground. Her nails dug into the soft earthen floor. The cat was really pushing its way out. Herman ran his fingers down her back and she shook as his energy ran through her once more.

"Is this something that happened because of me?" he asked.

"No."

He rested his hand at the small of her back and that forced a groan from her. She could feel her tail swishing as she sashayed her hips in the same motion that the cat would. The warmth of his palm burned through her skin and lit up all the pleasure points on her body. He moved his hand around the curve of her lower back and over her ass. She glanced up at him between pants and saw a light in his eyes. Either he was enjoying this too much or he was also turned on.

"What is it then?" he whispered, but she heard the need in his voice.

"I think you know what it is."

"It can't be. Your arousal is due to my healing interacting with body chemistry."

She scratched her claws through the dirt and bowed down, stretching out her limbs and sticking her hips higher into the air. His other hand touched her side, trailing along her stomach. He stopped himself before he caressed her breast.

"You don't believe that do you? You're just giving yourself excuses." The cat monitored their conversation.

"Do you want me?" she asked.

Herman's hand dipped between her ass until he found her already wet mound. A small whimper escaped her lips. This is what she longed for. All he needed was to mount her so she could feel his firm cock buried inside of her.

"Yes. But it would be wrong. You are hurt and — "

"Don't get all gooey on me now. Take me. Fuck me. Do it," she demanded.

"I could hurt you and shift."

"So could I. Please. I'm yours. Do it."

He did not wait another moment because he moved from her side and stood behind her. Herman ran his palm down the curve of her spine. She buried her face in the furs she had thrown on the ground and groaned. With his free hand, he cupped her breast and squeezed it until the pain was so sweet she nearly had an orgasm from it. When he twisted her nipple, she held on by the grace of the goddess. Herman said something that turned into a growl or it was lost in translation. He clutched her ass with both hands and ran his thumbs along the crevice between her ass cheeks before forcing her legs further apart. She grunted from the force, and wiggled her hips to urge him to keep going. To stop now would be sacrilegious. Elarna kept her eyes shut and focused on her breathing. The cat lingered right below the surface ready to arise. She licked her lips and felt the sharpness of her teeth as they had lengthened. She took deep, even breaths which didn't help because his scent permeated the furs.

He leaned over her back and the smoothness of skin had been replaced with fur that made her itch and shiver with anticipation. His claws dug into her hips as he gripped and pulled her closer to him. The hot throbbing length of his prick poked her ass. His tongue trailed over her shoulder and a blast of hot breath went by her ear. He grunted something. Her mounted her and pushed himself inside of her pussy.

"Oh yes," she cried out.

Having him within her satisfied some of the urge inside of her, but she wasn't going to be able to hold onto her shape. Already she could feel her body growing longer as he pounded into her. She backed her hips into him and flexed her claws deeper into the earth. His enormous length didn't bother her. She just focused on her anatomy and made sure they were compatible. Her bones popped and cracked as the feline emerged. Each time she groaned, it became more animal until she was hissing. Her tail swished in time with the urgency that he thrust into her. His claws raked down her sides. He grunted into her ear, but he didn't stop. Her change didn't appear to bother him. Instead, he seemed more excited. The cat in her needed to be satisfied. She gritted her teeth as everything in her tingled. Herman jabbed his claws into her flanks and roared. He stretched the length of her body, covering her from behind. Her nerves were on fire. As the pressure built, his teeth pierced her shoulder. Her pussy wrapped around his thick cock and held him while he released into her. Elarna yowled and felt the world fall away as an orgasm nearly blinded her. It racked her body until she thought she would pass out and left her breathless. It took a few minutes for her to recover as she swished her tail and regained her composure. Herman unlocked his jaw from her shoulder and flicked his tongue over the wound to clean it.

Elarna relaxed and she took female form once more. As that happened, Herman backed away from her. She felt better than she had in months. All the kinks had worked out of her body. She took a deep breath and turned around to see Herman looking at her with a satisfied expression on his face and a substantial cock still pointing at her, slick with their shared fluids.

She bent her finger and motioned him toward her. He did not move so she walked over to him and ran her fingers through his thick pelt, realizing it was finer than it looked. Underneath all the hair her fingers grazed over the indentions of all those muscles. The idea of being with him again inflamed her yearning.

"Thank you," she said to him. "I hope you didn't mind that I shifted."

He grunted, but she took that to mean no because he hadn't stopped fucking her.

"Good, because this time I want to be sure that you see my face." She trailed her hand down to his twelve inch shaft and wrapped her fingers around it. It would be a feat to take him into her if she couldn't shift. She was up for the challenge, especially when she could barely grip his girth in one hand. It was just a matter of shifting a certain part of her anatomy. She'd had bigger before. He wasn't as daunting as she'd thought he would be. Elarna planted her hand in the middle of his chest and pushed him down onto the furs. She was a little surprised that he relented. Herman grinned, showing all of his pointed teeth. She smiled back, took his claws and placed them on her breasts. He licked his lips. She straddled him and concentrated on her lower half and knew she had to alter it slightly. This time it was easier to access that part of her cat and her abdomen shifted until she could accommodate him.

Elarna slipped him inside of her and closed her eyes as his wide girth stretched her. It was pain and pleasure all wrapped into one, more than she had ever experienced before. He clutched her breast and pinched her nipples before twisting them. She rode him slowly, trying to draw him out. She had to swirl her hips so that he reached all of those buried pleasure points inside of her. Herman trailed his claws down her stomach gently, but they left a burn where they had marked her flesh. They settled on her hips so they could begin a rhythm. She twined her fingers through his long hair and took a hold of it, enjoying the pelt as she arched her back. He thrust into her and made her shiver. Elarna rode him, increasing the tempo between them. She threw her head back, letting the ecstasy of the moment wash over her. She dug her claws into his chest and realized they had grown without her feeling it. Each time he drove into her, she took all of his length. Each movement satisfied the animal instinct within her.

"Oh goddess. Yes." She roared and rode him until there was nothing more than them and the bliss of their union. He grunted. Herman plunged into her, and each time he lifted her up several inches. Elarna took a deep breath and opened her eyes. She was completely fulfilled and something between them had been cemented. She pushed her claws into his flesh and saw the desire in his eyes, the lust that burned them. He trailed his fingers over his stomach, sending tingles of rapture through her. He flicked his thumbs over her nipples and tweaked them. She cried out, and the orgasm sliced through her. A screamed ripped from her throat, and she came for the final time. Elarna collapsed on top of him contented, weaving her fingers through his thick pelt.

He laced his fingers through her locks.

"Was that good?" She looked into his eyes.

He nodded, and she saw that he was satisfied just as she was. And no matter what he might say, there was something between them. It wasn't something caused by him healing her.

Chapter Four

Herman watched her lavender breasts rise and fall. It relaxed him to hear the little snort that came out when she exhaled. After their lovemaking, she had fallen asleep. He half expected her to fade back into a dream. And yet Elarna had remained. At first he was sure that she would balk at his length, but she had only wanted more of him in both forms. He never thought he would have a mate. If he had been normal, he would have had four or five mates to wait on him or to even cohabitate with another male and female. It happened at times that bonds were formed with other family units. It didn't matter to him if he had a male or female sexually. He was attracted to both sexes of his kind. Nevertheless, he was denied a family because of his abnormality. None wanted it passed down to their children, even though it was a genetic mutation and they needed a healer. It didn't seem to matter. This violet fleshed alien had crash landed into his life and now everything was turned upside down.

He thought back to their lovemaking and how it had felt to be inside of her. It was rather a strange thing because she had transitioned her shape to accommodate him. Her features had taken on a more animal appearance. He hadn't expected it would arouse him, but it did. At first, he thought her attraction to him was because of the healing he had performed. He became emotionally connected, and it heightened the patient's arousal until it wore off. But it hadn't worn off with Elarna. She was a beautiful specimen, and he wanted to see her complete animal form as well. It didn't appear she had shifted entirely when they had mated. His desire stirred once more, thinking about the firmness of her body. He ran his finger over the smooth flesh, and warmth settled over his heart once more. Her injuries were not completely mended. Her anatomy was taking longer to heal than he was used to.

He was rather reluctant to want to finish because once she was well again, Elarna would wish to go off with her hairy companion and search for the other woman that had been in their ship. Herman assumed the royal guard had found this other woman and brought her back to the city. Phillip was worried for their friend. He shook his head and thought about what the guard would be doing to her. They would take the alien and use it for medical experiments, interrogate it, and then torture it until it had no more use. If the other alien wasn't already dead from the crash. If Elarna was found, the same would happen to her. Phillip, he might be able to pass off as a distant cousin, because there were some similarities between them. If a Yetan needed healing, they would discover Elarna. He couldn't hide her forever. He growled and slammed his fist into the ground. He had to keep her out of harm's way.

Someone coughed, and when he looked over, Phillip stood in the doorway. He made a gesture for Herman to follow him. Reluctantly, he got up from Elarna's side, but not before pressing his muzzle to her forehead and kissing her quickly. She stirred in her sleep but did not open her eyes. That was good because she needed rest more than anything right now. His healing could wait. He walked into his living quarters and put another long leg bone on the fire. Against the cave wall, a pile of luma stones glowed faintly blue in the light as they absorbed the heat. Phillip stood by the stack, picked one up, and inspected it before putting it down a few moments later. The other male may not have been as tall or as muscular as Herman, but there was something about him.

A strong energy surrounded Phillip, a connection to the world around him. If they got through this all alive, then he would inquire with the male.

Phillip clenched his fists, but he reverted to his skinless shape. Herman did the same so they could communicate.

"What is it you wanted?"

"I didn't mean to interrupt, but you seemed finished."

Herman chuckled. This male knew enough not to disturb him when he had been mating with his woman. "She didn't invite you to join in so I went along with her cues."

"I understand. I had the same thing happen with Alika. Although, I never figured how it would go. My wife…" he stopped in the middle of his sentence. A flash of pain crossed his features as his eyes crinkled before he looked down.

"Wwifff." Herman tried to mimic the sounds Phillip had said, but it was nearly impossible for his throat to make the word. What came out was a breathy whistle.

"Sorry. Mate."

Herman understood that and gestured for the other male to continue.

"On my planet, on Earth, we marry, take a mate for life, but my original mate died. I was left alone for a long time until I met Alika. Elarna's friend, the one who has gone missing. She and I are mates so you can understand why I want her back. I can't let anything happen to her."

His eyes widened. This confirmed the other in the ship was a female. He hadn't been sure. He certainly did understand why Phillip would want to save her. The pain was even greater in his eyes, more recent. It mixed with the rage as he grimaced and bared his teeth. "Elarna is not my mate, but through my healing, feelings have been shared. I don't desire anything to happen to her either. I can't put Elarna in danger. You must understand that."

"I do. So what do we do?"

He paced around the fire, thinking. His eyes trailed over to a small alcove carved out in the cavern he tried to forget was there. Maybe it was time for him to pull it out again. He had sworn when he left the city he would never return. His mother had begged him not to leave, but it was best for all of them. She had cried; the look on her face and the pain of her heart breaking was something he lived with for a long time. It was the right thing to do. He had brothers and sisters enough to take up his duties. Herman walked to the niche and removed the luma stones from the top of the hide that hid the chest. A few crystals rolled along the floor and hit the fire pit rocks. It had a musical sound to it, but he ignored it because it brought back too many memories of his youth.

As a boy he had been proficient in the Crancok horn. His father had killed one on a hunt in the southern regions where it was slightly warmer with more vegetation. The creature stood on eight legs and weighed more than three tons. Its bottom teeth protruded over its jaws. It had leathery skin and a long tail with a barb on the end of it. The horn grew out of the back of its skull and curled around its head like a loose fitting collar. The more coils in the horn, the older the beast. The one his father had killed had spun around the beast's neck five times, making it nearly five centuries old. The horn and the hide were taken as a trophy for his father. The Crancok was stuffed and set for all in the castle to see. A three foot section of horn was sawed off and holes drilled into it where he could place his fingers. When he opened the trunk the Crancok horn was the first thing he saw. He trailed his fingers over the holes. It had taken years to master because it was one of the hardest to play. He set it aside and looked under the cloth that hid the other contents of the trunk. Under the array of clothing his mother had made for him when he was in his hairless form was the sash that identified him among the other Yetans. It wasn't practical for him to wear clothes in his normal form so they draped sashes across their bodies to ascertain position and rank. Elarna would need to wear clothing. He moved the clothing aside and pulled out the band.

"What's that?" Phillip asked.

"It's the way of getting into the city and past the guards without them suspecting anything. You'll have to come with me in your other form. We can say that you've come from the southern lands. Their pelts are darker than ours, almost your natural color. There are some other differences too."

"I don't look like you in your natural form. They'd guess that we are different species."

What Phillip said was true, but he rifled through the clothing and found a cloak. "I have another idea, but you're going to have to keep your human form. Can you do that?"

The other man sighed and eyed him. He sensed Phillip's distrust, and he didn't blame him. He detected something else about him too, but it frustrated him because he couldn't pinpoint it. He would rather be in Elarna's arms, but there was nothing he could do about that. He didn't know how to process that he was already falling in love with the lavender female in his bed.

"It'll be difficult. If the sun is up, then it won't be a problem. But once it sets, I will be turning back into the Bigfoot. Since this is a different world with three suns, I'm not sure my curse knows how to work here. Alika was teaching me how to control my animal side. I don't know if I can hold the human side for a long period of time."

"It is a matter of being calm with the animal inside," Herman said. "I might be able to help you with that when there is more time." A shock went through him when he touched Phillip's arm. The alien male stared at him. He locked his gaze with the naked man and even with his pale pinkish skin, he was still attractive. Herman caught Phillip looking at him and for a moment he was sure he felt the same magnetism. He had helped to heal him even if it was a minor injury

"What are they for?" Phillip gestured toward the garments.

"I can bring you in to the palace as my apprentice. In a healer's garb, I can go anywhere. Even in your beast form, if you stay covered, which this cloak should accommodate both forms, you can come with me. It does for me when I wear it. To get there, we have to travel underground. It is not the most direct route, but it will keep us concealed from the guard who fly overhead and take us to a back entrance that isn't patrolled often."

"Sounds like you've done this before."

"Not exactly. Become your Big Feet, and we will go."

Phillip nodded and Herman wandered back into the other room. Elarna was sound asleep and purring. Her face had flattened some, and a slight golden sheen had appeared on her face mixed with her lavender flesh. He ran his finger along her cheek and it felt like smooth feathers. How could he have been blessed to find someone so beautiful that wanted him and it didn't bother her that he had two forms? She had even been able to take all of his size and it didn't hurt her. It seemed they could enjoy one another in either form they were in. He wondered if...

Herman shook his head and pushed the different ways of making love to her from his thoughts. Instead, he squeezed her shoulder and shook her gently. She opened her eyes and flashed him a sleepy smile. With his hands on her, he could feel the slight injuries that she had left, but it was something he could avoid. The urge to heal her did not overwhelm him.

"Hey." Elarna sat up.

"Hi," he pushed a strand of hair from her eye. "I need you to do something for me."

"Sure."

"I'm going to take Phillip to rescue your friend."

Her expression darkened. "I'm coming with you. If Alika's hurt, you're going to need some help. I…"

"No. You can't. Listen. The guards will be flying overhead looking for other wreckage or survivors. You have to stay here. I don't think they'll come into the cave because the guard knows who I am. If they do, go into the main room and to the left of the fire pit is a tunnel. You probably won't even know it's there. It looks like a wall. Go there all the way down. You'll come to some old stone steps. They lead to the ruins of an ancient temple. There are many places to hide there; no one will find you. Take one of the luma stones." He gestured toward a mass of crystals in the corner. "Blow on it and it will light up."

"You can't go by yourself."

He brushed her lips with a quick kiss. "I'm going with Phillip. I'll bring your friend back here no matter what." *If she's alive or dead.* He couldn't bring himself to say the last part.

"Thank you. Once you bring her back, maybe then we can figure out how to get off this ball of ice."

Herman stood, and her words echoed in his mind. She was going to leave him. He couldn't think of that now. He had given his word that he would help Phillip. "There is food and water in the main room. The blankets will keep you warm and there are a pile of bones to burn next to the fire."

"Okay." She grabbed his arm when he tried to leave. The look on her face made him stop. "W-What if you don't come back?"

Her dread filled expression and the small lines that deepened her eyes stopped his heart. Maybe she really did care about him rather than this being a fluke encounter. "I'll be back. I promise and I'll bring your friend."

She nodded. He left and walked out to the main room, feeling the transformation come back out on him so he had taken his normal form once more. Being with these aliens had given him more time to spend in his hairless form. Herman could come to like that form, and he understood why Phillip chose to like it as well. From what he gathered, the hairless visage was the normal shape for the other male. He was pale skinned and interesting to look at. Herman grabbed a pack that he stored his clothes in and the cloaks he had set aside for himself and Phillip. They would need it when they were close to the palace.

He glanced at Phillip and gestured for him to come. The other male nodded. Herman took a few luma stones and handed them to Phillip. He led the way along through the tunnels that he had walked many times over. This time he prayed he would be able to get in and out of the castle without any trouble.

Chapter Five

Phillip followed Herman. As he did, the the earth underneath his feet helped to anchor him. The thought of being in Alika's arms drove him onward, following the large white haired alien who had opened his cave to them and had offered his help. He was surprised that a relationship or something had formed between Herman and Elarna. He was getting to know the violet skinned alien more on the ship, but he wasn't expecting the crash. He still wasn't sure how that happened.

Either way, he knew that Herman reminded him of the stories told on Earth about a Yeti. It was bad enough he was called a Sasquatch or a Mud Ape, depending on where in the world he was at the time. If there were other BigFoot like him on Earth, then maybe they had the same abilities he did to tap into the elements and not leave a trace behind. Maybe those men had been cursed as well. In his case, he had fallen in love with a shaman's daughter, and he had been cursed for it. Phillip had been doomed to roam the world alone, forever. Nothing could hurt him that he knew of. He had been shot, stabbed, part of him had been blown up; he'd fallen down a mine shaft, been impaled, and always he had come back from it. The man who had put the hex on him made sure that he would live out his eternity as a beast by night and a man by day.

Then he found Alika, and his world had changed overnight.

Who would have thought an alien and a former human cursed to be a beast would end up together? Now he was on another planet filled with Yeti who wanted to dissect the woman he loved. One of their own was trying to help him, and he also could turn into a man or at least what Phillip thought of as a man. As he thought about the man underneath all of it, Phillip felt an odd stirring within him. It was an attraction to the other man. He'd had his run-ins with men and women over the centuries. He'd had to become compatible, and sometimes he had slept with a man. For a moment he thought of the other man and what might happen between them.

He shook his head and needed to focus back on finding Alika. Phillip would have to maintain his human form for as long as he could. His rhythms were thrown off here. He wasn't sure if it was because of the three suns or just because it was a different planet. However, if it meant being human for Alika then he would do it if it killed him. Herman was not so comfortable in his hairless form. They had to be careful because Phillip didn't want to find himself on the examining table. He couldn't describe what he was to these space yetis, and the last thing he wanted to do was end up in a zoo. That was the thing that he had feared about getting caught on Earth. How could he explain how he transformed back into a human at the rising sun? Who believed in magic? Over the years, he had met only a handful of believers, and the ones who had tried to help him were unsuccessful in removing the curse. Maybe it was supposed to be that way. Maybe he was supposed to have helped Alika the way he did. Now he was a Bigfoot exploring space.

He had been astonished finding her because her footprints had resembled a wolf's, but they had turned human, and he had found her passed out at the foot of a mountain. The sun was rising, and hunters had seen the ship sail across the horizon and ignite the treetops. He remembered the expression on the scientists' faces when he had come out of the forest with Alika. They were surprised he had any intelligence. What would they think now he had landed on a planet full of alien yetis? He chuckled, and the sound echoed through the cave.

They had been walking for a couple of hours. Some places he had to crawl on his hands and knees, but if Herman was able to go through the tight spaces in his furry shape then so was he. They emerged in an ice cave. The purple sunlight bounced off the walls and made everything lavender. The way the ice had been formed it looked like swirls of various colors, and he was caught in the middle of it. He marveled at the cavern's beauty and would love to show it to Alika. He pictured her green skin bathed in the lavender light and how tantalizing she would look.

Herman grunted and gestured that they had to move on. He nodded and continued walking until the other male put up his hand for him to stop. Herman's form shrank, and he became the hairless ape. He took the pack from his back and handed Phillip a cloak and some other clothes as well. It was time for him to work on being human for as long as he could. Once he was, he slipped the clothes on and caught Herman's gaze on him and saw something in his eyes. He wasn't sure how to read it. Phillip pushed it off and pulled a shirt over his head. The garments were too big and so were the boots, but they were warm.

"How far away from the castle are we?" Phillip asked.

Herman sighed and cracked his knuckles. "Just down the hill and around the corner. It's not far. This will bring us to a side entrance to the palace. It isn't heavily guarded."

"How do you know about it?" Phillip asked.

The yeti ran his hand through his white hair. "Because it was the entrance that my mother set aside for me so I could come and go without the guards questioning me in this form."

Phillip understood then that Herman was an outcast living in a cave away from others. "Why did they send you out of your home?"

"Being in this form, while I can heal, it's considered an abomination. Everyone in my family except my mother looks at me as though I am deformed. It was easier to leave and have others come to me if they need healing. My father could barely be around me because I was the reminder he had created such an aberration. My mother tried to get him to understand, but he wouldn't listen. It was easier for me to leave and get in touch with my wild side. This curse is heredity through the male line. Even though the healing ability is considered a gift to our people, the transformation is considered a scourge."

He laid his hand on the alien's shoulder. "I understand completely. On Earth, BigFoot are nothing more than myths or at least that is what people like to think. Earthlings are not able to shift into any other form. I got the way I am because I pissed off the wrong girl's father two hundred years ago, and now I'm eternal as far as I know. So I understand being alone and not having anyone in your corner."

Herman laid his hand over Phillip's. A jolt rushed through him. He looked at the man's green eyes, leaned forward and pressed his lips to his. Phillip wasn't sure what had come over him, but he went with it. After a second, Herman returned the kiss and pulled away.

"I didn't realize you were attracted to males."

"It depends on the male," Phillip replied, aware of the coy tone in his voice.

"Good to know, but we have to worry about getting your female out from the palace before we think about ourselves."

"Right. Sorry. I don't know what it is about you, but..."

"It's because we shared energy. I tried to heal you before. If this attraction you feel remains, we can act upon it later.

Follow me. Keep the hood of your cloak down and don't say anything. If you are asked a question, just grunt, act like you don't really understand what the guards are saying. You're my apprentice. It won't raise any alarms because I was sent far away to the southern regions where healers are more prevalent and accepted. Understand?"

Phillip nodded and knew this was it. "What if I shift back?"

"Do the same."

"If you're just learning to channel your ability, then it will be understood. It took me a while to learn how to hold my hairless form." Herman walked up the embankment to the cave opening.

Once outside, Phillip saw the town below and a larger building that spanned half of the town. Other Yetis strolled the streets, but he didn't think about anything as they walked the open expanse because all his concentration was on maintaining his humanity so he could at least try and be whatever it was Herman wanted. He pulled the cloak over his face and trudged through the snow toward the city, following the yeti. They got to the wall, and Herman stopped before a metal door. It was dull black with a few spiral designs in the metal along with an elaborate chevron. Herman pressed the gate in a specific pattern among the diamonds. They lit up one by one until it clicked and the door swung open. Phillip followed into a garden with plants that touched the top of the wall. Phillip looked out from underneath the hood and tried to keep from revealing any of his face or form to the other tall beasts. The floor was constructed of the same metal that the door had been. It was also etched with designs that looked like snowflakes.

As they entered the hallway, Phillip held his breath and prayed Alika was alive. Herman led him through twisting hallways that appeared to be carved directly from the ice.

Along the walls were various types of stones that he had encountered in Herman's cave that gave off enough light they could see by. Windows were carved into the ice. Several yetis walked by, all carrying spears, but they didn't give them a second glance. He kept his gaze down and tried to stay underneath the cloak and prayed they would not make him stop. They came to another door guarded by two sentinels. He glanced up at them, and they resembled Herman in his animal form, all in white, but they each had a green sash draped around their shoulders with medallions on them. Phillip figured they signified some kind of rank. They crossed their spears together before Herman and grunted.

Phillip listened to the growls and the sounds uttered between the three Yetans. It all sounded menacing. The translator didn't work between beast and human. He wasn't sure because the one Alika had implanted was broken, and they hadn't gotten a chance to install a new one. He would like to understand what Herman was saying to the others. Even with a humanoid throat it was somewhat difficult for the alien to speak the guttural language. It took a few moments of them going back and forth until Herman lifted his hood and then gestured toward Phillip. They seemed disturbed by what they saw and pulled away from them. The guards uncrossed their spears and let them pass into the other room. So far Herman had kept to his word, and they had gotten inside the compound.

Phillip hoped they wouldn't find the woman he loved strapped down to an operating table and being probed. If he ever did end up back on Earth, he could tell the people there that aliens weren't what they thought they were. At least he hadn't encountered any thin, gray aliens, who pulled people up in a beam of light. He couldn't say no about the implants because he had some alien piece of technology shoved into his head. When he walked inside of the room, they were in some kind of a viewing room.

From his vantage point, he saw Alika strapped down to a long metal table with medical instruments spread out on a tray beside of her. One of the yetis said something to her, but she shook her head. He inserted a long needle into her head, and she screamed. Phillip started to go find a way to get to her, but Herman grabbed his arm and shook his head. The fury at seeing his beloved being tortured was a knife to his own heart. All he wanted was to barge in and rescue her. Her cries echoed through the small room and grated on his nerves. It stirred the beast within him, and it took all his control not to change back into the Bigfoot. He couldn't take on all the sentries, rescue her, and get out of there if he showed his true self.

Herman whispered. "I know you want to get her, but you're going to have to trust me. Follow and stay behind me. Understand?"

"Yes." Phillip flexed his fingers and forced the beast into its cage in his mind. It was like wrestling a bear, but he made sure the beast was in the back and waited for Herman.

Chapter Six

Herman glanced once more at Phillip. The other male wrestled with holding his other self back because he wanted to rush in and free the green skinned female lying on the examination table. He had to act quickly to get her out of there while there was only one scientist. Herman stared at the tabletop and shook at the memories that enveloped him: being strapped to that table and enduring the probing of the needles because scientists had to study him to see if he had different anatomy than the other Yetans had because he could switch his form. Cold fear had overtaken him in those moments. Herman had cried out for his mother. The first change had come over him at nine when his friend had been hurt. He hadn't understood what had happened to him. All he knew was he had a duty to help his friend. Herman had healed Urmaran, but at the cost of losing everything. After that incident, his father had him examined by the scientists. The head of the Institute of Science was a ruthless Yetan who wanted nothing more than to advance his career. When they were done with him, Herman remembered not long after another craft fell from the sky. He had snuck into the viewing room and saw an alien on the table being tortured and studied exactly the same way the green female was.

It had to stop.

Her cries filled his heart and sparked the healing instinct within him. The longer he waited, the more Phillip was in danger of transforming back into his other form. He curled his hands into fists and stood straighter. He might have been an outcast, but he was still the prince and that had some weight.

Herman pushed open the door to the laboratory. The other scientist spun around to confront him. "What are you doing here?"

"What exactly are you doing to this poor creature? Can't you see that she's in pain?" Herman walked over to Alika and flashed her a small smile. He wasn't sure exactly how much she could see because her eyes were clouded over with drugs and one was milky white where they had blinded her. The agony radiated off her like heat. She had been bandaged in some places, but he sensed she was dying. There had been some internal damage done either from the crash or from what they had inflicted upon her. She didn't have much time. If her anatomy was the same as Elarna's then it would take him several sessions to be sure all of her wounds were healed.

"I-I...I was told to finish the tests before we disposed of her. We are almost done with her. Then she will be taken for vivisection."

Herman held in his temper. He rushed around the table and began undoing the metal cuffs that held the alien down. As he undid each restraint, he noticed bruises laced over her flesh. He glanced up at Phillip and saw him shaking. He tried to hurry. The scientist sputtered as Herman took off the last manicle and found a sheet to wrap Alika in. Her long, purple hair spilled over his arm as he held her close to him. His body tingled as he mentally took stock of her injuries. One of her hearts was injured, but both remained beating. One of her lungs wasn't working, and there were various drugs within her bloodstream. They had tampered with her reproductive organs.

"This is inhumane. I don't care about your orders. I'm returning her to her cell to give her the proper care that she needs." Herman walked out of the laboratory and back into the viewing room. Sweat dripped down Phillip's face. They had little time before he transformed back into his other form.

Phillip reached out to Alika. "Is she…?" He choked up with emotion.

Herman felt for the other man, knowing he loved the female. He could see it in his pained expression and how he held out his arms for her even. "She needs a lot of healing, and that means we have to get her out of here. Come on." He slipped out another door concealed in the viewing room he knew wasn't guarded. He pressed a code into the door to open it and slipped through. Phillip came with him. A small sigh of relief passed over his lips, knowing that they had made it past one small obstacle. There were bigger hurdles still coming. He turned and observed the small room. He gazed down at the viewing room. He held in a growl and stepped into the greater room, his parents' chambers. He laid the female on the heaps of luxurious hides his parents slept in.

"We can't stay here," he insisted. Phillip knelt beside her.

"I know, but she's in no condition to go anywhere. If we move her too much she's going to die. I have to stabilize her before we head back out into the cold." Herman laid his hands on Alika and tried to substantiate which were her worse wounds. The most life threatening were the drugs in her system. They were shutting down her organs slowly and compromised her immune system. A virus had been injected into her bloodstream. It left a copper taste on the back of his tongue. The heat flowing through him was something he had to focus into her. Getting the drugs out of her was problematic and dangerous. The only way he could do it was to make her sweat them out. Once he cleared her system out, he could work on making sure she was whole.

"Can you help her?" Phillip kissed Alika's left hand. She muttered something in her native tongue.

"I can try. Go in the other room and let me know if you see anyone coming in."

Phillip hesitated, but then he left Alika's side. Herman closed his eyes and focused on the toxins within her blood. He concentrated on raising her body temperature. It caused her two hearts to beat quicker. She began to pant, but soon she was sweating the poisons out. They turned the hides pale blue. He felt the dirtiness and grittiness of it all within him as well. His body warmed up as he fought through the changes within her metabolism and tried to keep her alive too. Alika cried out. He gritted his teeth from the amount of energy he expended. Perspiration ran down his nose and his hands.

"Herman, someone's coming." Phillip warned, but he hardly heard him.

The other man thundered into the other room. He tried not to panic, but his heart sped up and Alika's raced as well. If he pulled out now, he would hurt her. There was nothing he could do to stop working on her now. If he could get the drugs from her body she would have a chance and he could focus on balancing her other systems out.

"Heragthan, what are you doing here?" The high pitched voice made him look up to see his mother had entered the room. Phillip stood behind her with the cloak thrown back over his head. "What are you doing w-with th-that she alien?"

"Mother, I'm saving her life. It's hard to explain. They were treating her horribly. I had to come. I was called here. You know I don't have any control over it at times."

His mother walked over and touched Alika's face. He saw the sympathy in her eyes. The hair along her crown had been braided with small chevrons. The top of her pelt had been dyed brown to accentuate her eyes. Other trinkets had been woven along her chest into something of a shirt to cover her breasts, and the charms jingled when she walked. Smattered among her fur he noticed the silver hairs, but he also sensed something else. She was pregnant once more. She was too old to be having children.

"Oh, Mother," he said.

Her eyes widened, and she trailed her fingers over her stomach. "It was a surprise. You know your father."

"I do."

"Then you know he'll kill you for treason for interfering with the alien. I can't have that happen to you. Please leave her be before the alarm goes off."

Herman shook his head. "You know I can't do that. She needs medical attention. Did father tell you that she is also with child?"

His mother's eyes widened, and small moan slipped from her, her way of showing sympathy for the alien female. He glanced at Phillip who seemed stunned and then anger filled his eyes. Herman saw his skin rippling. He hadn't known about the child. Herman just realized when he said it that was the anomaly he had felt when he first touched her. She was very early on in her gestation, but he was not sure if the fetus had been damaged because of all the experimentation performed on the mother. He hoped he could save both.

"Oh, dear. He didn't tell me, but it shouldn't matter. She's dangerous. Her kind takes our males, spiriting them away in the night to do monstrous things to them. You know this."

"No. They only take men who are willing to go with them. They don't take those with families of their own. Alika explained it to me." Phillip went to the other side of the bed and took her hand.

Herman believed him, but he also knew that his mother saw Phillip take her hand and when she saw the expression on his face she would understand there was something between the other male and the green female. He wanted to say something else, but all of a sudden he heard the stomping of footsteps outside in the hallway and knew the alarm had been sounded. The palace was aware the captive had escaped. He had to be sure that they got out safely. He needed to get back to Elarna and be sure she was okay.

He reached across Alika and clutched his mother's hand. "Please Mother, we have to leave here."

She looked between the three of them and her eyes settled on Phillip. Herman knew she had not understood what he had said. "What's going on really? Is he one of them? Is he one of the aliens that crashed in the ship? What is your father going to say?"

"Mother, Phillip is Alika's mate. They crashed with another female who I have come to have feelings for. She accepts me for who I am. I love her. We need to be able to get them off the planet. We need your help."

She turned to Phillip. He prayed she would be able to read his mind or at least understand what was going on with all of them. "Is it true, you are one of the aliens?"

Phillip looked at him and he translated what it was that his mother had said. Phillip nodded, picked up Alika's hand and placed it over his heart. His skin wavered as he was trying to hold onto his shape. Herman had an idea that might help his mother understand what was going on.

"Transform into your other form."

"Are you sure?" Phillip asked.

Herman nodded.

He sighed and laid Alika's hand back down on top of her chest and quickly stripped his clothes. His mother gasped at the sight of the naked man because he was different than the others. He was pale, and there were only five toes on his feet. But he still did look like a male. The sight of him again stirred his desire, but he pushed it aside and thought about the task at hand because they had to get out of there. He should be thinking about Elarna and not his own yearnings for the other man. His mother gasped, watching the change. She looked back at him.

"He is like you?" she asked.

"In many ways, yes. He is not able to heal others, but he can heal himself quickly, and he can understand what the elementals are saying to him. He's told me his story. There are things that he can do that I've never seen before. These women that came with him can also shift their forms. We can't just slice them up. He is from another world where all his people are hairless. Wouldn't it be better to learn from them instead of pumping them full of drugs, cutting them up, and then using their parts for healing tonics? Please. We have to get out of here."

She touched her stomach once more. When she glanced back up at him, Herman saw the compassion in her eyes. Once he had her interested, he knew she would be on his side. She sniffled and crooned something at Phillip before looking down at Alika. She placed her hand on top of Alika's head. Herman heard banging on the door.

"You're Majesty, please open the door. The alien has escaped," a guard yelled through the door.

"Mother, please," Herman begged, and grabbed her arm.

She pulled away and went to the main door. She opened it, and he heard the conversation. "Thank you for the warning. I'll let you know if I see anything."

"Ma'am, can we come in and search your rooms?"

She lowered her voice and he was not able to hear the rest of their discussion. He glanced at Phillip and he fought to switch back into his other form. He wasn't having any luck. He held up a hand and gestured for him to come to the edge of the bed. "You need to be here with her. Alika is going to need your strength. Can you understand me right now?"

Phillip nodded. He trailed his fingers down her cheek carefully.

Herman squeezed his hand. "I know you didn't know about the baby. I'm sorry. I hope that I can…"

The other male growled something, but his mother came back into the room. "Heragthan, your father is not going to be happy about this. I can't hide the three of you. The guards who saw you, the scientists will talk. Whoever saw you… You can't stay here. They'll come to your cave and find the other woman you're hiding. The guards will go out on another patrol. You won't be able to stay *here*."

"Where can I go?" he asked.

She rushed over to a trunk in the corner where she kept all of her ceremonial jewelry and attire and dug into it. She came out with a metal tablet and handed it to him. "This will show you the way."

Herman glanced at the tablet and his eyes widened. "You know what this means?"

"I do. Your father doesn't know about this. He's never known. It's been protected by my line. Go out the back. I'll distract them the best that I can." She drew him into his arms and gave him a quick hug. "Never let anyone tell you that you're not worthy of the gifts you've been given."

He nodded, unable to find the words to respond. He handed the tablet to Phillip who had donned his cloak and it covered his beast form. He shot him a questioning look, but there was no time to explain what was going on. Herman scooped up Alika and held her close while also taking another fur from the bed and wrapped it around her so she would stay warm in the frigid environment. He gestured to Phillip to go out into the garden next to his mother's quarters. They sneaked out, and the plants were larger and more overrun than the small courtyard where they had first come into the palace. His mother screamed something to the guards. They clamored toward them. They would have to go around the rest of the palace. Once they passed, he pressed a series of buttons in the wall, and a panel slid back. Herman could see his exit. If they could get around the bend and out of the open before the others noticed, then they would have a chance to get into the caves. No one knew the cave system like he did. He glanced back at his mother but didn't see her. A pang of sorrow hit his heart because this was goodbye.

They dashed from the compound and slipped out into the open. As they did, he heard the blaring alarm. They moved as quickly as they could through the snow drifts and into the cave. Above them, Herman heard the distinctive sound of wings cutting through the air from the guard searching for them. They tread further in as he saw the first shadows of the winged creatures fly overhead. Alika's breathing was shallow, and he didn't want to put her in anymore danger, but they had to press on until they were out of sight. The guard would see their tracks in the snow, unless another storm had blown in and covered them. So Herman led Phillip an alternative way back. This would give him some time to stabilize Alika without being interrupted. He would have to work quickly so he could get back to Elarna. Phillip knelt next to the female and held her hand. Herman laid a hand on his.

"It's going to be okay. Hang onto the tablet and let me know if you hear or see anyone coming. I need you to let me work on her. Once that happens then we can get back to Elarna. Then we can talk about what is on that tablet. Okay?"

The other man nodded and stood up, keeping the tablet next to him. Once Phillip was out of range, Herman concentrated all his attention on Alika. Moving her had not helped. It had thrown her systems out of synchronicity, so he had to make sure everything was working congruently once more. Her breathing was labored. Her hearts beat erratically. Something was wrong with her spleen. He gritted his teeth against the work ahead of him and let his hands guide him to where she needed to be healed. He tried to get her body back in a harmony with itself.

Chapter Seven

Elarna lay snuggled in the furs that Herman had left for her after he had departed with Phillip to rescue Alika. She prayed to all the goddesses she knew they would retrieve Alika and get her back safely. She hoped her friend wasn't beyond helping. *I wonder if his ability to heal is passed down through his family. That's how it is on Rovan with our healers. Sometimes there are things that technology can't heal. If it is, it would be a great asset to the planet. Although when I mentioned going home and getting off this ball of ice he didn't seem too happy.*

She hadn't assumed he would want to go, but maybe he did. He had seemed to share her attraction to him. He didn't discourage her when she made advances toward him. They had consummated their relationship, but it could have also been in response to the physical need she had within her. Nonetheless, her hearts warmed when she thought about the gentle giant. He had saved her life. It was at least fair to repay him in some way.

Whenever he was around her, Elarna's head swam with the sight and the smell of him. His animal scent triggered her desires. Maybe it was something to do with the energy that had passed between them or maybe it was a pheromone. Either way, the Yetan had been kind to her and was risking his life to save her friend. She had traveled to the farthest corner of the universe to some backwater planet to rescue Alika. Not that she minded because her friend had gotten her out of many tight spots in the past, but Elarna never figured that she would find a male in all of this. Or that she would crash land on the hunk of ice that was forbidden because of what they knew about the planet.

The planet had been put off the list for the procurement of males because many years ago a distress was picked up. A woman had landed on Kraztarn and the Yetis were waiting for her and her partner when she got off. Her partner made it back in wounded, but she sent out a warning that they were taken hostage and doing experiments on them. It wasn't safe for anyone to come down to the planet. Someone had gotten into the ship and had killed her. Now their ship had been destroyed in the crash. She had no means of getting home. They would be on the run for the rest of their lives. How could she survive on such a hostile world for the rest of her life?

Something clattered to the cave floor and echoed through the cavern. Elarna held her breath and remembered what Herman had told her. She listened again and it sounded again. The sound of feet crunching stone. The clothes Herman had set out for her were on the edge of the bed. She slipped those on. The shirt was too big and hung to her knees. So were the pants and the boots, but at least they were something to keep her warm. His words went through her mind as she tried to stay calm. Elarna took a couple of luma stones and wrapped a fur around her so she could stay warm. She poked her head out and didn't see anyone in the main room. She found the animal he had killed and wrenched a leg off it and took a bite. Elarna hugged the wall as she inched down the corridor and heard low growls coming toward her. She recalled the entrance for her escape might not look like an opening at all. The stones scraped along her back as she inched further down until she found a niche to hide in.

It was then she saw the other Yetans.

If they were in the cave, then they must have figured out Herman was the one who had taken Alika. The large, hairy beasts grunted, and she prayed they would not see her. Elarna blew on a luma stone as Herman had said to do and it lit up in the darkness. She could see further down the tunnel as it declined deeper into the earth. The others said something; they sounded closer. She had no time to spare. Elarna descended as quickly as she could and discovered a long staircase that went further down into the ground. She couldn't see the end as she kept on going, and the air grew warmer so she didn't need the pelt. But she wasn't about to drop it in case the guards came looking for her. The luma stone only provided enough illumination for her to see a few steps in front of her. Everything was eerily quiet; she could only hear her pulse pounding in her ears and her breathing. She stopped what she thought was half way down to catch her breath. She had to blow on the luma stone again to make sure it stayed lit. It was clear the stairs were ancient because some were chipped and appeared cracked, but she wasn't too concerned and finally made it down to the bottom. When she did, she was met with a large stone carving of some creature with its mouth wide open. Herman's warning rang in her mind. There were hiding places in the temple that she should find.

The crystals gave off enough light to examine the temple. It appeared to be old. If it predated the evolution of the Yetans, then whoever had carved it was an advanced civilization because of the precision of the carvings and how tightly the stones fit together. She ran her hands over a column that stretched upward into the darkness. Maybe the race had been giants because everything around her was massive. The writing on the pillar was faded so she couldn't make it out.

Utter silence surrounded her except for her footsteps reverberating around where the temple resided. It didn't seem like it had sunken into the ground by some earthquake. The structure seemed intact. Elarna walked down a large promenade with statues of wolf like creatures lining either side spaced about every ten feet. They appeared to be alive, staring at her. Their teeth were barred and several of them had two tails. She placed her hand on one just to make sure it was cold stone. The further she ventured into the temple, the hotter she got. She was sweating with the fur and set it behind one of the stones, out of sight. She realized that she was heading toward something. This was not just a temple, it was an underground city. She just didn't know how large it was because she didn't have enough light to see by. From the main promenade she saw more hallways that went left and right and diagonally, more than she could count. There appeared to be openings to homes, but she wasn't sure.

Instead she kept on going straight until the road ended at the steps of another building. Elarna went up the steps and found that she was in what seemed to be a large temple. Curiosity drew her into the bowels. She headed toward the altar and saw two doors on the side. The right one was closed, so she went into the left one. She blew on the luma stone and it brightened some. In the center of the room was a statue of a Yetan. Its arms were outstretched and the fingers pointing in different directions. Which direction would bring her to the temple's inner sanctum? If this was a place like some other cultures she had come across then certain tunnels could lead to traps or nowhere at all. Or they could be a labyrinth. A draft of air blasted from her right she decided it was best to go in that direction because the air was fresher.

As she walked down the corridor, she noticed a painting along the wall. It was a mural of a Yetan reaching out to lights in the sky. There was another being who resembled Alika with green skin, but the features were not defined. As she moved along the mural it depicted the Yetan and the other alien mating. A child was born and then the green skinned alien left the Yetan with the child. On the next panel, the child was elevated in status. The Yetan held the babe and pointed toward the stars. The next panel depicted the child laying hands on a Yetan, but he was hairless. The last one showed the child older, hairy and he was still held in reverence. Her mind began to work at the things she had seen. The statues of the two tailed wolves looked similar to Alika in her canis form. On Rovan they had healers who could shift into an animal. The painting showed a green skinned woman coming out of a spaceship. It was too much of a coincidence.

"That's interesting," Elarna muttered. Maybe the child was some ancestor of Herman's because he was special among the Yetans even if he didn't see that. He healed and technically had a dual nature. If he carried Rovian genes that meant they were related and it also showed that the procuring of males had been going on for longer than anyone knew. *I wonder if he knows about this. If not, he should.*

The corridor she was in came to a sudden stop. At the end of the passageway the orangish red glow of lava lit up the space. The room had a large crack in it from where the stone had fallen into the magma. It was obvious that she was in a volcano. There was no telling when it would erupt. From the size of the chamber, it would be a colossal disaster when it did. She couldn't see to the other side of the mammoth lava lake. Elarna glanced upward into the volcano's throat and saw the blue and purple light of luma stones that resembled the night sky with the stars winking in and out. Half way up was a ledge that looked large enough to land her ship on, if she still had a ship.

Elarna stayed by the lava pool for a while and enjoyed the silence while eating the leg of the animal Herman had cooked. It had a tangier taste to it than what she was used to, but she enjoyed it. She wondered if she was okay to return to the cave and see if Herman had come back. She couldn't have them be captured. She couldn't have all of the work he had gone into healing her and them rescuing Alika go to waste. She decided it was best that she go look because maybe he was searching for her as well. Elarna headed back down the corridor, retracing her steps.

As she walked, she noticed hers were the only footsteps in the dust that had settled onto the floor. When she got past the mural, she heard someone whispering. Creeping closer, she gripped the luma stone ready to use it as a weapon. It was the only thing she had besides shifting her shape and she didn't want to be caught naked if she changed back. If she needed to communicate it was easier to be in human form. She slid along the wall and peered around the corner. Alika leaned against the Yetan statue wrapped in a long fur. Her friend looked tired, as if she had been through all the under dimensions, but she was walking around. Alika stepped into Phillip's arms. Elarna glanced at Herman who had switched back to his beast form. He smelled like something she had never detected before. It was an intoxicating mixture of musk and something with a darker edge to it. She knew it was safe and came out from around the corner. When she did, she stood before him and bit her lip, realizing how awful she must look. He smiled at her. Her reservations melted away and she hugged him.

"You got her out," she said.

He nodded.

"How did you get down here?" Elarna sked.

He withdrew a metal tablet and held it out to her. The writing on it was foreign, but it appeared similar to the script on the columns in the temple. She figured it must have been something significant. Maybe it was a map. "Can this get us out of here?"

He grunted which she took as a yes.

She walked over to Alika and placed a hand on her arm. "Hey, are you okay?"

The other woman chuckled. "Wonderful. I feel like a troop of gorenauts ran over me."

"Do you know what happened with the crash?" Elarna asked.

Alika shook her head. "No. I don't remember much except shoving Phillip into the escape pod and then we hit the ground. I thought I smelled something burning. It might have been an electrical fire. Something went wrong internally to trigger those sensors that went off. It wasn't like we were hit with something. Didn't I tell you not to stop at that outpost because they had cheap labor?"

Elarna chuckled. "I don't think it was the outpost labor that did it. I guess we'll never know exactly what it was. But it's good they got you out."

Her friend nodded, but Alika wasn't her chipper self. Something had happened to her that she wasn't ready to face yet or at least talk about because of the haunted expression she wore. She snuggled into Phillip who was in his Bigfoot form. Elarna went back to Herman. They couldn't spend the rest of their lives in the corridors of this temple. They couldn't go back up because of the guards. She hoped Herman had another plan.

"You were right about the guards coming to the cave. I came down here. Thanks for the hint. Do you know a way out of here? I assume it has to do with this tablet."

He nodded.

"Okay. Great. So I think we should go, don't you?"

He glanced at Alika and Phillip.

"I know. She's not all that well. I'm sure you did everything you could for now to get her up and walking the same way that you did for me. But we need to get moving. We can't stay here. If those guards come down here, they'll see my footprints and it'll lead them right to me." She waved the luma stone over the floor and showed him the footprints in the layer of dust on the floor.

He growled something. It appeared he hadn't thought of that. "There's something else I have to show you. I don't know if you've ever seen it."

Herman shook his head and pointed at another tunnel and then back to the main one she had entered the temple from.

"I know there isn't a lot of time, but it's important. Come." Elarna grabbed his arm and wrenched him down to the mural. "Look, it shows who you are and why you can change. This ship is almost like mine. If I were to guess, my people came here ages ago, and we joined with your people. Children must have been born. We have healers among our people whose lines go back generations. One of your ancestors was probably one of those children who could switch shapes. What you have is not a curse. I don't know what happened over the years, but once upon a time you were revered as a god. I suspect this temple was built, this whole city was built to house those like me and those who were born. Think about it. Somewhere down the line your people turned it into something bad. It also means that you should be able to control your shift the way that I and Alika can."

He ran his fingers over the wall. Elarna wanted to know exactly what he was thinking. He walked down the length of the fresco, stopped at the end, and studied the painting. She walked down to him and placed her hand on his furry arm, twining her fingers through his pelt and loving how soft it was. She stood up on her tiptoes and pressed her lips to his muzzle. Herman slipped his hand around her head and cupped it gently in his large hands before returning the kiss with a hungry one of his own. It was a little awkward because of his snout and his tongue was thicker than when he was human. He was just as attractive when he was like this than when he was a man. He pulled her into him and held her. She felt the hair recede from his body as his shape shifted, and he was the male with his dark skin and white hair.

"Thank you," he whispered, pressing his forehead against hers.

"You don't have to thank me. I wanted you to see that you don't have to be ashamed of what you are. That's all. Why didn't you ever come down here?"

He trailed his fingers down her cheek. "Because I was afraid. My father always told me demons lived within the bowels of this temple. I've never seen this. My father never talked about it and the past has been forgotten. They would never accept the fact that our people mixed with other aliens. How is that even possible? We're completely different species."

Elarna shrugged. She had only taken the basic genetics classes in school. All she had been told was that females were capable of mating with many different species and sometimes the genetics crossed over. It depended on the species and they weren't going after insectoid males. Those were not suitable matches, although they were an interesting species to sleep with. "It's possible. Apparently our inherent makeup is amiable to many other different species of alien and we bond well with others. I don't know the exact reason why."

"It's good to know. We really have to get out of here. If the soldiers decide to come down here, we won't have a chance to escape. I hope you meant what you said regarding me going with you."

"Of course I did. I just don't know how we're going to get off this ball of ice. Sorry. I know it's your home, but it's cold. I don't like the cold."

He held out the tablet and pressed a few places on the metal. It lit up. The technology surprised her. She had always thought Yetans were not so scientifically advanced. Seeing

CRYMSYN HART

that made her realize there was a lot she didn't know about them.

"What is that?"

"It's a map my mother gave me. It points the way to our escape. I can't sustain this form much longer. Healing Alika drained me, and she is not completely well. There was much damage done to her."

"What's at the end of the road?"

"A ship."

Chapter Eight

Herman processed the information Elarna had given him and what he had seen on the mural. He ran his tongue over his lips, tasting her unique sweetness and wondered why she had such an effect on him. He didn't want to let her go and knew she couldn't stay. He had to get her to the ship. He wouldn't see her hurt. But the thought of losing her tore his heart to slivers. He had no idea if the ship would fly. It was the only hope they had of escaping. If not, they would all be captured, and he had no idea what the guards would do to him.

He trailed his finger down Elarna's cheek, enjoying the softness of it. If he lost her then he would be set adrift. He had never thought he would find the one for him, but after the idea of not seeing her again and seeing how Phillip was so attached to Alika he understood what it meant for someone to love someone else. His parents had never truly loved one another. His mother had been given to his father to cement an alliance to the lands of the east where they needed to trade. His father never let his mother forget it, reminding her that he could always send her back no matter what. Seeing his mother pregnant saddened him because so late in life she could die from the birth if she didn't have a good healer there. What would happen if he and Elarna had a child together? What would it look like? Was the mural correct?

"I thought you said that we had to get going," Elarna said to him.

He nodded. The longer they lingered the likelier it was for the guards to catch up with them or for them to find the entrance to the cavern. One of the reasons he had set himself up in this cave was because his father had shown it to him. As a child, he had said it was important to their history and brought him down into the mouth of the great temple, but he didn't tell him about the painting. When Herman was dealing with his transformations, he had found the other entrance to the caves by the palace and navigated his way through the underground tunnels. The map his mother had given him had shown him more of an extensive underground system. It appeared that this had once been the entrance to a great underground city as Elarna had suggested. The past wasn't something that he was taught. He only dealt with the past few hundred years and how the tribes had all been warring until there had been a pact and how their line became royalty.

He touched her shoulder and led her back to the others. Phillip held Alika in the crook of his arm and it made him yearn for that closeness. It was something that he would love to have with Elarna. That wasn't going to happen if they were caught. Alika noticed him and smiled. His body reacted to her injuries as the warmth inside of him rose. He had done what he could to be able to make her walk again until they could settle down and he could heal her properly. In the time they had spent in the cavern, he had cleared the toxin from her system, but he was unable to save the child. Phillip worried about that, but they had decided not to tell Alika about it until she was well again. He prayed that would be soon.

He walked over to Phillip and pointed at the tablet. He nodded and seemed to communicate to Alika what was occurring. It had to be some other form of communication, maybe telepathy. Phillip picked her up, and she pressed her face into his fur. A pang of sadness struck his heart. Elarna was by his side, but he couldn't dwell on what might be. He had to get them out of there. He studied the tablet and thought about the way the statue was turned. He looked at it carefully and read the tablet again. There was something written about the statue and the way that it was pointing. It reminded him of the very last painting of the Yetan he had seen on the wall and it was pointing upward. None of the fingers were pointing that way. Something looked off about it. He touched the fingers on the statue and realized they could move. He repositioned all of them except the fourth finger on the right hand remained upward. Just like the Yetan in the mural. A click echoed in the chamber.

Elarna gasped.

The ground cracked around them as they slowly sunk downward at an angle. The luma stones lit up the passageway as they did. As they ventured down the tunnel, the heat in the environment rose. At the very end he could see an orange glow and the track they were on dumped them out into a lake of molten rock. They floated for a few minutes. The hot rock sloshed over the edges of the platform they stood on. It bobbed along with the tides of lava until it came to the over side of the pool. From there he heard more mechanics whirring underneath him. The stone rose slowly and the luma stones embedded in the walls reminded him of the night sky. They were the same configuration of stars he had seen in the painting. Whoever had painted the cave and constructed the tablet and the mechanism they were riding on were from a different time. They no longer had this kind of technology or maybe it had been lost. He had never seen anything like it. Yetan knowledge was advanced, but they wouldn't be able to build a spacecraft. This was their only hope in order for them to escape, and it seemed unlocking some part of the past was going to lead him to the future. They continued to the rise until they stopped at the top of a large shelf. Herman stepped off the elevator and looked around, listening for anything, but he heard nothing.

He gestured for the others to follow. Once they were off the platform, it slowly worked its way back down. He found a luma stone and pulled it from the wall. He swept it across the floor; no footprints marred the blanket of dust. Herman thought back to what his mother had said about the tablet being ancient and coming down from her line. If that was the case, then somewhere in his past her people had been connected to this place. That meant he was tied to it in more ways than he could possibly understand. As they walked down the hall, he saw symbols carved into the metal on the walls, but he could not read them. He stopped and motioned over Elarna, hoping she might be able to comprehend the language. He focused and moved back into his hairless form so he could speak with her.

"You know what these say?" Elarna glanced back at him and ran her fingers over the walls.

"Yes."

"It's an old Rovian dialect. I'm not sure about all of it, but from what I can make out, it tells how one of the leaders of our world came here. At first your people thought them to be gods. They taught the people here technology, building, etc. in exchange for males who were willing to go with them or mate with them here. Males from all over were sent here. They lived in harmony for several hundred years until a plague hit the Yetans. Unrest had been brewing for a while, and there was a revolt. The city was abandoned. Many were killed who could switch their shapes like the women who had come, but a few were spared because they could heal."

"That would explain a lot," Alika said; her voice was soft in the darkness, still filled with some pain. Her damaged eye was healed.

"What do you mean?" Hearing the history of his people it made some sense why there was a great distrust of him. People might not know now where it had originated, but it had lingered in the people's memory. This tale had been written by one of his ancestors. He wanted to know more about what had happened to the ones who had left and escaped the carnage.

"There are some on our planet that can heal with a touch. They don't know why because it isn't an inherent ability. It's valued, because sometimes the healers find stuff that the computers can't heal."

"Herman had asked me why they could mate with us, meaning why were our genetics suitable for one another, when we are entirely dissimilar species from different worlds. I wasn't really sure how to answer him." Elarna explained to Alika.

Alika sighed. "I'm at a loss on that one to. I just know that we're compatible with all the males that we have on the acceptable list that we're given as procurers. If we happen to find another planet that we haven't been to before, we try to gather a DNA sample to bring back and make note of the planet's position. If we are compatible with the population, then we can go back and introduce ourselves. Although I've never come across a planet that I haven't see in the database. Even Earth where I found Phillip. It's at the edge of our sweeps, backwater as it is, and we can mate with the males there."

Herman nodded. "Thank you for the explanation. I'm sure there's more to it than what you've said, but that is all we are going to learn here. Who drove them away?"

"It's too faded to tell. There is something, but I can't make out the writing." Elarna pointed it out.

Herman brought up the luma stone and ran his fingers over it, clearing away the dust. When he did, he gasped and backed away. The design was crude, but it was one he was familiar with. It was sewn into everything he had ever worn. It was on his mother's clothes and carved into the palace floor right at the main entrance. It was his family crest. Three chevrons at a diagonal all, their bottom points coming together. "I did this. My family was the one who was elected and drove the rest away."

"It was before your time. You didn't do this. Come on. Let's go see what's down at the end of this tunnel."

As Elarna led him away, he tried to fathom what his ancestors had done. He forced his body to stay in its hairless form and walked to the end of the passageway. A large door blocked their way. There was nothing on the tablet indicating how to open the door. Elarna studied the smooth surface and when she touched it, a purple hand print was left behind. However, the door didn't open.

"Try yours. I think it's DNA encoded," Alika suggested. "We have them on our ships."

Herman placed his hand on the metal. It was warm underneath his palm, and when he pulled it away, a yellow handprint was left behind. It took a moment. The door shook, showering dust all around them. When it opened, the entire room lit up. The dust on the floor and the stale air told him no one had been in this room for a long time. Once his gaze got to the object in the center of the room, he gasped.

"Oh my!"

In the center of the cavern was a large spaceship. If it didn't hold the four of them then there would be a problem. So many times he had thought about being among the stars. Anything to get away from his loneliness and the seclusion he had been forced into. Sometimes he saw lights moving in the sky. He had always wondered if those lights were intelligent. He grew up knowing the guard would examine anything that fell from the sky, but he had never really seen an alien until Elarna. He approached the ship slowly, feeling the fear building in him. He had never thought he would be scared of the prospects ahead of him.

"This is amazing," he heard Phillip say next to him.

"Yes, it is," Elarna replied.

"I haven't seen one of these since that field trip to the archives. This has to be at least five hundred years old." Alika walked around it. Phillip was by her side to be sure that nothing happened to her.

"Are you sure it's one of yours?" Herman asked.

Elarna nodded. "It is. It's just ancient."

"At least it proves that it was your people who were the ones who were here and not some other race. The writing could have been a coincidence."

"True." Elarna walked around it in awe.

"Do you think it will still fly?" Herman asked. "Can you fly it? I — "

"Over here," Alika yelled, cutting him short.

They walked around the ship to the other side. Lying on the floor were several skeletons that appeared to have been racing to the ship, but they hadn't made it. Instead, something had happened to them. He bent down and upon closer examination some of the bones had been burned. He didn't know any kind of technology that would do this. They weren't the bulky skeletons of his people and they didn't have seven toes. Herman assumed they were female. Elarna knelt down next to Alika. Tears streamed down her violet face and darkened her skin. Seeing those falling ice crystals around her cheeks was something that never should mar her perfection. He brushed them away and held her close.

Alika said something in a tongue he did not understand. It was obvious she was mourning the dead that hadn't gotten the acknowledgement they deserved. They were there for a little while until the females stood and Elarna smiled at him.

"Thank you," she whispered. She pressed her lips to his cheek.

"The hatch would be just about past here. I think they were trying to get to it when they were attacked. We should go inside. Look around and see if we can get this thing to run. If we can, then this is our ride home, and you're going with us," Alika stated.

He walked over to Phillip who had become his Bigfoot self again and waited while Alika trailed her fingers over the smooth hull.

The ship itself was made of the same kind of gray metal that was used in the palace and the tablet. It was oval shaped and domed on the top, but underneath it appeared to be flat and it hovered a foot off the ground. He didn't see any engines on the undercarriage of the ship. How were they supposed to get on it? As he thought about it, a thin metal ramp descended. He didn't see how it would support anyone, but the women walked up into the ship. As they did, he glanced at Phillip, and the other male smiled. Herman stood at the end of the plank, gazing into the dark interior of the ship and pondered what his next adventure would be.

Chapter Nine

Elarna stepped into the craft, still amazed this was buried underneath the earth all this time. This was part of her history and Herman's. This craft evidenced a time in their combined past that was important to both species. She had never been one for antiquated things and always worried about the future of the race. She had tested well as a pilot so she pursued it and then she was promoted into a procuring role. Elarna already had a ship so it was an easy jump. The craft before her might have been archaic, but as she took stock of the cargo hold, she could see some containers ready to go. If they were specimens, then they were all dead. However, what was more important was in the cockpit. If it was operational, then she and Alika could fly it. This behemoth was too large for only one person to fly at least until they got into space and could activate the auto pilot. Although, she wasn't too sure how well she would trust it.

"Do you remember where the deck was?" she asked Alika.

Her friend turned, but she still wasn't back to her normal self. Her emerald features were drawn, and her violet hair lackluster. They had met in school when they were children. Her skin coloring was unusual in their class so she was drawn to her because Alika's hair was almost the same color as her skin.

She forced a smile for her. "Through the door down the hall to the right. Engine room should be on the left. I don't remember anything else. It's been a long time. Let's see."

Alika touched a panel on the side of the door, and it slid open. They walked down the hallway with the luma stones to see the way. It was cold inside of the ship because it hadn't been fired up for a long time. She prayed that it would start so they could get off this rock. It was obvious Herman was coming with them. How would he adapt to being on their planet and having to be with other females? She could claim him for a mate, but it was their law he would have to couple with others. She wasn't sure that she wanted to share him with other females. Elarna had never thought she would come to find love. Even though it had been a short time of knowing him, she realized she did love him. By the way he took in everything, he seemed overwhelmed. *How can you blame him? In such a short time he's learned that his shape shifting ability came from a union with our ancestors.* His ancestors were the ones who had driven them back and had potentially killed the people that had brought technology and new skills to their planet.

Outside the next door were several mummified corpses. Burn marks marred the door to the bridge. Weapons lay scattered around the hallway. It appeared the three were trying to break down the door and get inside. Herman knelt down before them. He sighed and then shook his head.

"I don't know how they died, but they are Yetan. What do you think they died from?" Herman asked.

Elarna shook her head. "I don't know. Some kind of gas maybe. It's hard to say without getting into the log to see what actually happened." She stepped around the bodies and placed her hand on the control panel. It took a moment, but the door opened. She went into the cockpit and discovered two skeletons in the pilots' seats. Elarna studied the main helm. Comparing it with her ship, it was more spread out and some controls were further apart. It didn't look too foreign for being antediluvian. She prayed the startup sequence and the levers to jump the engine were in the same place. Alika stood on the other side of chair, and they looked at one another.

"This is a dual control system. They haven't had this in three generations," Alika stated.

"Are you going to be able to fly it with me?" Elarna glanced at her friend.

The other woman flashed her a smile and the twinkle in her eye made her look like her old self. "This old bucket of bolts? Of course I can fly it. This thing has to learn how to deal with us. How about we fire her up?"

"We should move them first."

Elarna nodded. They were going to move them when the males came over and lifted the bodies from the chairs and set them down in the corners. Elarna trailed her fingers down Herman's cheek and watched him shiver and return the smile. She focused her attention back on the helm and found the ignition switches. Alika did the same. In this old kind of system both pilots had to be working together. They had to be a team, and if they didn't trust one another, they could never fly the ship. They pressed the normal initiation sequence and nothing. They looked at one another. Her hearts dropped into the pit of her stomach. They weren't going to be able to get off the planet. The whole craft quaked, and the panels lit up on the helm. The whir of the engines was a glorious sound that made her hearts sing. The rest of the ship came alive.

"Are you going to be able to go back to your home world?" Herman asked.

She turned toward him. "There's enough to get us home. All four of us." She walked over to him and twined her arms around his neck before pulling him close. She kissed him gently and the sense of relief that she had overwhelmed her. "We have to figure out how to get out of here. I'm not sure how the cavern opens. I think we're supposed to go up through the funnel of the volcano, but if we do, it might trigger an eruption. I don't want that to happen."

"And if it's the only way that we can get out of here?" Herman asked.

She looked at control panel, hoping find a log to inform them what had occurred on the ship. Nothing.

"Alika, why don't you go through the ship and see if there is anything we can salvage. I doubt the supplies are going to be useful. There is an outpost a day from here where we can resupply. They owe me. From there we can make the run back to the planet. I need to find the log. It's going to take me some time though. Herman, why don't you and Phillip go with Alika? She can give you a tour."

She glanced at her friend, who rolled her eyes, but nodded. Elarna needed some time to figure out what the craft was made of and how they were going to get out of the middle of this volcano. The two of them went with Alika. She sighed and looked at the bodies. Elarna hadn't wanted to tell Herman what had happened before. The ship was equipped with a defense system. It was triggered as a last resort. A lethal gas released within the ship had killed all that was on there. It looked like this was something that they had done in the past to prevent the Yetans from getting in and possibly taking over the ship. Elarna thought back to her control panel and pictured it superimposed over this ancient one. It was very similar. The buttons were in different order, but as she pressed a few of them, a holographic screen flickered on. She studied it. It was easy to understand the gauges and how much fuel they truly had. The levels were a little lower than she had first suspected, but it would get them off the planet and to the outpost so they could refuel.

She studied the last plotted course and star charts. They had come from Rovan. She breezed through the rest of the star charts, and they had more planets in them than she had seen before. Whatever the reasons were, these worlds had been wiped from her database. If she read the charts right, the ship was older than she thought, over a thousand years; much could have happened in that time period. She swiped her hand over the holographic image, and it moved so she came across a video log. The woman sitting in the chair had green skin like hers, but her features were further apart and her hair shaved close to her head. She sighed and sat back in her chair before looking into the camera. It took a moment before she spoke.

"All the negotiations have failed. The Yetans have starting killing those who have come here. War has broken out among the clans, and they are driving out anyone who is unlike them. Even those born with our genes and can shift. Any who have a different tint to their fur as well. We have offered to help, share with them any information they might want, but they don't want our technology. They want us gone. They've chased us back to the ship. Others, if they haven't been killed, they have been experimented on. We've waited as long as we could for the others to come and seek refuge. Only a handful made it. The Yetans followed them into the ship. Now they're beating on the door. Serva was hit badly when I came on. She's already dead. I could pilot the ship by myself if I needed to, but it would be problematic. It would bring me to the nearest settlement so I could refuel and save the others, but the Yetans are already banging on the door. We just wanted them to understand that all we want to do is have children. It is difficult for us to claim one of them as a true mate, but sometimes it happens. They're firing on the door trying to get in, but there is no way in. Their laser guns don't have the power to get through the metal. All of it they have learned from us and yet…" She stopped and shook her head.

"There's no other way. The others will understand. I can't let them overtake the ship. There has been too much death already. Over a thousand years of peace between us gone in just a few months. Maybe one day someone will see this and understand why."

The image flickered. The aviator reached over and pressed a button on the helm. The vision died when the captain slumped back into her chair and went silent. Elarna knew the gas had taken effect. She wiped the tears from her eyes. When they got home, she would finally put these women to rest. If there were others on the ship, they all required a burial.

She pressed a few more buttons on the control panel. One triggered the hull's shield to open so she could see more of the chamber they were in. And it was also lit so she could see the funnel of the volcano. Another hologram popped up, showing the maze of passages and the structure of the tunnels and the city. There were fifteen docks for ships and three remained besides the one they were on. She couldn't tell how many were functional. Maybe the Yetans had found them and were studying their knowledge. It didn't really matter because they were getting out of there. All she had to do was get Alika back into the cockpit, and they could be off to the station. Elarna ran her fingers over the board once more and was going to start the launch sequence, but felt a draft of cold air waft across her back. She paid it no mind at first and then heard a voice.

"Turn around slowly, and I won't shoot you."

Her blood ran cold as she heard the gruff voice and realized that the ship's translators were working because she wouldn't have been able to understand the statement if they weren't. She turned as instructed and found a large Yetan holding a gun, pointed at her.

"What do you want?" This was not something she had foreseen. Elarna had figured they had lost the soldiers when they descended into the lava pool.

He pulled out a small tablet and pressed a button. A picture of her three companions popped up on their knees before an older, white haired beast wearing a purple sash. This had to be technology they had gotten from her ancestors. "If you want to see them again, come with me."

She nodded and started to get up.

"Slowly."

Elarna lifted her hands to show him she wasn't armed. "I'm going. No need to be rude."

She walked before him out of the ship and into the hangar. They were surrounded by ten soldiers all with different types of weapons and in metal armor. At the other end of the warriors was the older Yetan with the purple sash and she assumed it was Herman's father. The king.

"My, my. There is another one of you, and you're the same color as one of our suns. How strange is that? Are you the one my son has become infatuated with? I would think that was the only reason he broke into our facilities and rescued this green one here," the king said to Elarna.

"Leave her alone, Father," Herman grunted.

She glanced at him and saw a look of pain curl his muzzle. She couldn't see a wound, but that didn't mean he wasn't hurt underneath all his fur. It was interesting to hear his voice and recognize what he was saying. It was brusque and growly, but she yearned to hear him say her name in that wonderfully husky voice of his when he was in his beast form. She just had to replace her translator and then she would be able to understand him in any form. Elarna hadn't tried yet to read his thoughts, but then again she hadn't shifted completely because of the situation that she had been in.

"So it's true! You do have feelings for her. I supposed it does make sense, considering she is an abomination just like you."

"What you call an atrocity saved her life and probably many more on your planet," Phillip barked.

One of the soldiers bashed him in the stomach with the butt of his spear. The Bigfoot doubled over. Elarna glanced at Alika. Her friend seemed to be in some pain and a fresh cut ran across her face. She didn't want whatever happened to her friend to end up happening to her. None of them were going to be experiments, lying on a metal table, with them poking and prodding. By the look in the king's eyes he was thinking the same thing. The king glanced at Phillip and laughed.

"This one is an interesting alien. He's almost like us, but not exactly. We'll have fun dissecting him and seeing what makes him tick. However, we're going to keep you around because you seem to know how to fly these crafts. We've been hoping to find someone like you."

"I'll never show you how to pilot these ships. You won't ever get anything out of me."

The king looked at her and bared her teeth which she realized was his way of smiling. "If you want my son to live, then you will."

Chapter Ten

Phillip glanced around and took in the situation. As Alika had been showing them the ship, they had come across more bodies in some of the rooms. Many of them had appeared to be her kinswomen, and she had needed a moment to clear her head, so they had stepped back into the hangar. Once they disembarked, they were surrounded by the guards and Herman's father. Herman and he had gone back and forth in a growling match until one of the soldiers hit Herman. He stumbled and had fallen, clutching his chest so Phillip wondered if he had cracked a rib. Alika had tried to go to the ship, but one of the guards had hit her again, slicing her cheek open.

It took a moment, but he realized the arguing snarls turned into something he could understand. *There has to be some kind of translator within the cave so I can comprehend what they are saying.* It was difficult not being able to understand what they were saying half the time and being in his human form when he wasn't used to holding the shape. He glanced at Alika and seeing her hurt all over again burned him up inside. It killed him that he couldn't help her. The thing that really hit him was that she had been pregnant and because of all the damage done Herman wasn't able to save the baby. The loss lingered in his heart. He never thought he would ever have the possibility of a child because of his curse, but Alika had shown him anything was possible. She was his. He studied Elarna and saw her gazing at Herman and wondered if she felt anything for the Yeti. Sure they had slept together, but that didn't mean anything, considering the first time that Alika had sex with him, she had wanted to thank him for saving her from the crash that had occurred on Earth. He wondered if Elarna had done the same for Herman, but judging by the look in her eye, he figured she had feelings for him. Whatever the feelings between all of them, something had to be done to get them out of there.

Alika, Phillip thought at her. He prayed her converter wasn't busted and she could hear him.

I hear you, she answered him.

They don't know about my unique abilities. Don't be alarmed.

He could feel her trepidation, but he didn't see any other way. Phillip reached out and felt the power of the earth still there and it answered him. *I need your help once more. Shake this place as hard as you can,* he implored the element.

It took a moment, but the ground quivered in response. It trembled; the guards stumbled. The quakes became so violent that one toppled over and pushed Herman backward. Phillip leaped at the Yeti closest to him and tackled him so he fell to the ground. He got up and roared at the others. Herman seemed in a daze. The next tremor was so violent large rocks crashed down around them. The others jumped back to get out of the way of the falling pieces. Smaller debris hit the guards on the head. Herman got up and glanced at Phillip.

"Back into the ship!" Phillip shouted and prayed that the translators were still working. It seemed they were because Herman nodded and made a dash back toward the ship. Elarna was there. Phillip felt a burning pain in his side from one of the guns that the Yetans shot at them.

"Stop them!" the king shouted. "We can't let them get away."

Phillip reached down and picked up Alika, cradling her in his arms. She snuggled close to him. He stumbled when another searing spear reached up his back. It was getting hard to breathe and to see. The earth was no longer connected to him. Another tremor hit, and it cracked open the ground. The chasm split before him, and he jumped over the groove. When he did, something hit the center of his back. He lost his step and nearly fell, but he miraculously kept Alika in his arms. He went to his knees and when that happened, he let Alika out from his arms.

"Go ahead," he forced out.

"I won't leave you," she whispered.

He breathed through the pain and the numbness that lingered in his legs from the last shot he got. "I'll heal. You need to get in there. I can handle them." He gritted his teeth and turned toward the Yetans behind him.

Only a handful were left, shooting across the gap. Herman was saying something to his father. The old man wasn't looking. There was another shake, and the gorge grew bigger. The ground gave way underneath the Yetan king, and it sucked him into the earth. Phillip looked down into the gorge and saw the red lava beneath. It rose faster than he had anticipated. The others had stopped firing and were fleeing, trying to escape the cavern. The earth crumbled beneath his feet. Alika tried to come over to him, but he shook his head for her to stay where she was. He tried to grab onto the side of the chasm, but his fingers were slipping. The heat of the lava burned the soles of his feet. If he was consumed by it, he would never come back from it. He was about to slip into the abyss when a hand enclosed on his wrist. When he looked up, Herman was there holding onto him.

"If I let you go, I think your lady would have to kill me," Herman said. He hauled Phillip back on the ground and onto his feet.

"Thank you," he muttered.

"We need to go," Elarna shouted.

Phillip glanced at Herman one last time. When he felt the last shake, he realized there was nothing that was going to stop the oncoming eruption. He hadn't known by asking the earth to help him it would awaken the volcano.

They raced up the gangplank into the belly of the ship. He glanced back and saw that the ramp was closing and they were sealed within the vessel. They got to the bridge, and Elarna and Alika sat in the chairs. They were pressing buttons and sliding their hands over the metal of the control panel. He looked up and saw the hangar outside. He was going to say something when the whole ship shifted, and he was thrown forward and onto the panel.

"It's time we get out of here. The volcano is going to erupt. When it does, it's going to flood all the interconnecting tunnels along with the city. Everything that our people built, including the ships that have remained behind will be lost," Elarna said.

"Perhaps that is for the best," Herman whispered.

Phillip glanced at him and laid a hand on the other male's arm. He was sure knowing that and what was to come was difficult for the Yetan because he was watching the possible destruction of his city. Elarna said something underneath her breath, and then the ship quaked until he had to grip onto the seat. It took a moment, but he felt the engines propel them forward. The wall opened up before them, large enough for a ship to pass through. The lava filled the hangar. It was going to blast them and consume them if they didn't get out of there. As the cavern separated to free them, he saw blinding whiteness and nothing else.

"Ready?" Alika asked him.

"Let's go."

The vessel throttled forward and they shot out of the hole in the mountain until they hovered over the city. He looked down as they panned and black smoke poured from the mountain.

"We can stay and see what happens," Elarna said to Herman.

"I'm sure your mother will be okay," Phillip remarked.

"No. Let's just go. And yes, she'll be okay. She'll be a better ruler than my father ever was. It's time to make a change." Herman stood by Elarna's chair and touched her shoulder.

Phillip tried to think about the universe that was out there and the planet of Rovan they were going to. What was it going to be like when they went? Would he be able to keep Alika as his mate? He knew that he didn't want to be with any other women. They flew upward, going out of the atmosphere until the violet sky disappeared. They were out of the atmosphere, and Phillip was staring at the purple sun. He marveled at the sight before he felt the engines kick in and they were left with nothing but other stars to gaze at.

"Alika, you should go with Herman and have him finish looking at you," Elarna said.

"I'm not going to leave you to pilot this tub by yourself."

Elarna waved her off. "I'll be fine. One pilot and auto pilot will be able to fly the ship. You need rest."

"I'll keep you company," Phillip chimed in and flashed the other woman a smile. "You can teach me how to fly."

Elarna opened her mouth to say something, but then closed it and nodded. "Sure. Have a seat, and we can figure this out."

Phillip took a seat, and he heard the door open and close. He ran his finger over the panel, careful not to touch any of the buttons. "Do you think this ship is going to have any problems like the last one?"

Elarna threw him a dirty look. "I don't know what happened on my ship. The only thing I can suspect is that it had some type of electrical problems. But we'll never know the true cause of it. But I can't help what goes on with this ship. It's ancient. I hope we can get to the outpost. All the gauges say the systems are working and the engine is fine, but we will see. Pray the goddess will grant us the ability to get there safely. What did you really wish to speak to me about?"

He stared at the stars and wondered which one they were hurtling to. "I'm worried that when we get to your planet I'm going to have to give up Alika. She's told me of your practices that you share your males with other females. You procure males from other planets and spread them out among the populace."

Elarna sighed. "Not exactly. There are some who enjoy the thought of multiple wives or lovers. Others donate their genetic material so that the females can be impregnated. It all depends on the male and the female. You wish to have Alika all to yourself?"

"Don't you want Herman all to yourself?" By her long silence, he figured that the answer was yes.

"There is no me and Herman. He was gracious enough to help us and..."

"He sacrificed his city and his family for you. I'd say that was a pretty good show of devotion to you."

"Are we here to talk about me or you? Because I've also seen the way you look at him. Don't tell me you are attracted to him?"

Phillip smiled. "Not in the way you are, but I'm curious, and there is a physical desirability. As he said, it's probably because of the energy he had shared with us."

"Have you thought about..." she looked at him and it appeared she was blushing. "Being with him?"

"The thought had crossed my mind. It isn't anything that I haven't done before. I haven't been completely celibate in my isolation. When I am a man, I have been with other men before. I have been alive for over two hundred years because of the curse put on me."

"Do you think that will change now that you're no longer bound to your planet?"

The wounds he had suffered from the guns were closing so his condition hadn't changed. "No. I know it hasn't because my wounds are healing."

"What about with your children? Do you think it will transfer to them?"

"I don't know and before now I never thought the idea was possible."

Elarna laid her hand over his. "You are an honorable human, Phillip. What you choose to do will be respected. My people won't force you into a lab to be studied. I'm sure they might ask you about your planet and how it is you are the only who can do this. They will ask you for your DNA, but they won't compel you. There is a processing center where we'll have to go, but it doesn't have to be right away. They will want to do a medical examination on you to be sure you aren't carrying any contagious diseases. They'll probably replace your translator at least then we should be able to understand you away from the ship. In the end, you don't have to worry about not being with Alika."

"I'd like that. How long have you and Alika been friends? I never asked you before."

"Since we were small in school together. We've always been close in more ways than one." She winked at him.

He smiled. "I thought you only had eyes for the big, white Yeti."

"I may, but that doesn't mean I haven't looked at you either. I had inklings when you first came on board, but you are attached to Alika. Although it might be something we can discuss."

"I'm not used to women being so forward."

The door opened and he looked behind him to see Herman had come back in. He was in his male form, and he looked weary. "Alika is resting, but she is well once more. There was a lot more damage than I had anticipated. Their anatomy is so different it takes a little longer for me to work on her. Go be with her."

Phillip got up and pulled the other man into his furry embrace and hugged him close. Once more, the strange attraction he had for him arose. "Thank you."

He left the bridge and let the two of them be alone, thinking about everything Elarna had told him. Phillip thought about the woman he loved. It made him warm inside and being so close to losing her was something he would never let happen again. He found the quarters she occupied and slipped inside. A panel next to the door was lit up where the others were not. He found her stretched out on a large bed with a blanket covering her naked form. He slid in next to her, embraced the male inside and the beast receded so he was all man to her. Phillip snuggled into her, feeling the warmth of her body.

"Phillip," Alika murmured softly.

"Shh…you need to rest," he said and kissed her neck. Being with her like this, it was easier for him to be a man because he could relax. He ran his finger over her stomach until his palm rested on her chest in the space between where her two hearts beat. She turned over and pressed her forehead to his. Seeing her smile made his heart sing.

"I don't need rest. Just to be with you."

"I'm here with you."

She trailed her hand down his cheek. "You saved me."

He shook his head. "Herman saved you."

Alika laughed. "You know that's not really how you pronounce his name?"

"I know, but I can't say his name right even with the translator. There are some things in your language I don't quite understand, but I get the gist of our conversation. I think he realizes that. I know I'm not saying your name completely right either. It flows off Elarna's tongue much better than mine. I do have to admit something to you though."

"Anything."

"Going to Rovan, Elarna told me what will happen. I know what we've talked about me being with other females, but I don't want you to ever think you're not going to be my first choice if or when that happens."

She threaded her fingers through his hair. He loved her soft touch and still couldn't believe that she only came up to his chest when she stood up, but in her canis form she could reach his shoulders. Alika was a magnificent woman. "I know that. There are things you'll have to endure, but I know you're always going to be there for me no matter what happens. Don't be surprised that you'll have females bringing you gifts and trying to bed you. It will be a whole new life that you don't ever have to think your existence is a curse."

"How do you feel about sharing me?"

"I might not enjoy it, but I understand. It's the way our world has been for thousands of years. And no matter what, I know you'll always want me."

"I love you, Alika."

"I know, Phillip."

He pressed his lips to hers and kissed her lightly while she cuddled into his arms and soon fell asleep.

Chapter Eleven

Herman waited patiently while Elarna went into the outpost that they had landed at. It had been two days since they had arrived. They had all been together for a week. Herman thought about the loss of his father, but it didn't bother him. His father had already written him off years ago. He prayed his mother had escaped the volcanic eruption. He was sad for his people being caught in the blast, but the more he was with Elarna, he understood this was where he was supposed to be. He was in love with her.

It didn't matter that she said it was better for her to go in alone because the ones inside were leery of new people. The longer she was away from him, the antsier he became. When she returned to the ship, he was in the cargo bay waiting for her. Seeing her walk in, he forced his beast form away and then he had her in his arms. Herman caught her up and pressed his lips to hers. She stiffened in his embrace until she melted and pulled away from him.

"What was that for?" she asked.

"I don't like it when you're away from me."

Elarna chuckled and patted him on the chest. "I wasn't gone very long. Besides, I have to get back in and pilot the ship."

"Once we get going, I was hoping we could be alone."

"I'm sure we can arrange that." She pecked his cheek before heading toward the front of the ship.

Herman followed after her and into the bridge. There he found Phillip leaning close to Alika and whispering into her ear. He was hairless and Herman felt that connection to him more than he ever had. He wasn't sure if it was because they had shared energy when he had tried to heal him or not. And Herman had a desire for Alika as well. The drive was there but it was more so now that he was in his hairless form. If he didn't act upon it, then it would only grow. Phillip glanced up, caught his eye, and threw him a smile. He felt his cheeks burn at the image of Phillip and Alika in the same bed with him. Recalling the quick kiss he and the other male shared stirred his passions the same way that Elarna did. Too much bombarded his mind regarding the idea of his coupling when he felt Elarna put a hand on his arm.

"If you're thinking what I think you're thinking, the answer is he's interested as well."

The statement surprised him. When he looked into her eyes, he saw the mischievous grin as well. "Really? And what about you? I wouldn't want to upset you."

She trailed her fingers down his chest. "I would be joining you. If that's something you want to explore."

"We'd have to ask them. Can only one person fly this ship? You said before it took two."

"The autopilot can compensate for a time. The more I've flown it, the more Alika and I have discovered about it. So yes we can assign it for some time to keep on the right track. All we have to do is ask them."

She went over to the other chair and pressed a few buttons. Phillip kissed Alika. Herman watched and wondered how it would feel to have them against him. His heart beat a little faster as he studied the male. He had never been forward before with another male. But his healing had linked them together. Elarna would be with him. Herman walked over and trailed his fingers along Phillip's arm and saw the shock in his eyes. Phillip broke his kiss from Alika. He stared at him, but didn't move. Herman took a deep breath and touched Phillips's cheek lightly and captured his mouth.

Phillip kissed him swiftly, but Herman brushed his tongue along those silky lips before pulling away. Alika stared at the two of them as though he had done something inappropriate in front of her. "I'm sorry, I should have…"

Alika shook her head and laid her hand on his other arm. "There's no need to apologize, Herman. This happens on Rovan very often."

"That is good to know. I can't help it. I thought it was something to do with all the energy that I have shared with you because of healing you, but this attraction is stronger in this form than my beast form. However, I wasn't sure how you would feel about it."

Phillip nodded. "I know what you mean. I've been questioning it too, but if the girls are up for it, then I'm game."

"I think we just have to decide on whose bed is big enough," Alika said.

"I found just the place." Elarna grabbed Alika's hand and pulled her into the hallway. Herman flashed Phillip a smile and went after them. If this was going to happen then he was not going to question or regret it. His woman was in for it and so was Alika. He walked down the hallway. Phillip and found the room the women were in because the door was open. He stood in the doorway and observed them on the bed. Their lithe bodies were pressed against one another as they ran their fingers over one another's flesh and kissed. Phillip said something he couldn't quite understand, but he figured it was something that showed off the awesomeness of the view before him.

Herman felt his cock firm at the sight. Phillip pushed past him into the bedroom and also stopped. Elarna traced her fingers down Alika's green physique. Alika drew the other female closer and kissed her and cupped those purple breasts. A small groan left his lips, and Phillip took in a quick breath. He looked over and saw the other man's shaft was as hard as his. The muscles bunched in Phillip's back. He touched those, and Phillip turned from the spectacle on the bed. He smiled at Herman. Before he could pull away, Phillip planted his mouth on Herman's once more. This time the kiss was smooth and filled with desire. He wrapped his arm around the other male's neck. He closed his eyes and pressed against the Earthling. His body was taut, and he realized he was taller than the other male, but that didn't matter. He ran his hands over Phillips's side until he fondled Phillip's prick. The kiss was broken off as the other male uttered a soft moan.

Herman moved his hand faster along the other male's dick. Phillip planted small kisses along his jaw. He shivered with delight and sensed more warmth along his back. When light fingers trailed down his spine, he realized one of the females was behind him. Wet lips pressed along his shoulder blades as hands moved along his spine. Phillip had stopped kissing him, so he assumed another one of the females was working on him. Those small kisses turned into nips, and he couldn't hold in the groan. He opened his eyes and saw Phillip's head thrown back in ecstasy as purple arms wrapped around him and her nails trailed over his pecs. He caught Elarna's eye and felt a small spike of jealousy go through him, but she flashed him a smile that promised the things to come later. Alika's fingers played with his nipples and twisted them. He gritted his teeth at the pleasure that rushed through him. He wasn't sure how long he could hold out. Her tongue licked along his spine. It was rougher than it had been before like sand dragged across his flesh.

Elarna gripped Phillip's balls and rolled them around in her hand. Herman watched with fascination as her purple fingers were such a contrast against the other male's pale skin. It was the same with Alika's against his black flesh tone. Phillip thrust his hips forward and moaned. Alika grabbed his ass and squeezed it. Herman curled his toes and tried to keep his control. The bliss of her touches was already creeping up on him. The beast within him stirred, and he had to keep it contained. It was the first time he remembered actually trying to keep it shackled within him only because it too wanted to experience the ecstasy. It was as though he was feeling this for the first time as a separate part of him and not together the way he always was with the beast. He rocked on his feet with the petite female who was touching him. She slid around him until her breasts pushed into his chest, and she flashed him a perfect smile. Her teeth seemed to be pointier than what he remembered. She walked her fingers down until she cupped his prick and slid her hand along his sensitive skin. "Ghrysts…"

Alika giggled. It was an intoxicating sound that sent quivers through him. "That didn't translate, but I don't think that was you saying you're not having a good time." She stood up on tiptoe and nibbled his bottom lip. He captured her head and held her, winding his fingers through her hair.

"I don't know the words in your language for coupling. But I need you. Now." With his other hand he clutched her ass, lifting her leg so it curled around his hip. She moaned as he lifted her up and pressed her against the wall. For a split second, he thought about being too big for her, but when he slid his cock inside of her depths, he felt her shape shifting. She grew taller and her body elongated in all the right places.

Alika growled something as she kissed him harder. Her teeth caught his lip, drawing blood. The hot taste of it slid down his throat. It drew out his inner beast more, but he was able to ignore it for now as he thrust into Alika. He kissed her with a hunger and let the passion of the moment take over him. Her nails dug into his shoulders as she held onto him. He cradled her head so it wouldn't hit the wall, but each time he moved all of his length into her pussy, its firm walls gripped him and she met him with the same frenzy. The energy they had shared between them was there as well. He could feel his connection to her, and in a way also experience her mounting pleasure. Herman found himself focusing on that as well as his building enjoyment.

"Yes. More," Alika screamed.

Her whimpers encouraged him, but when he heard another husky voice in the room, it drew his attention. He saw Phillip nestled between Elarna's legs, pleasuring her with his tongue and his hands. Herman watched for a second the techniques the other male was using and saw Elarna enjoyed it as her hips rose and fell and her cries filled the room. However, before he could watch her climax, Alika's exaltations drew him back to their act. He kissed her again and looked into her eyes, noticing they were golden. The shape of her face had changed. Her claws pinched his flesh, and the pain mixed with the desire of his act rushed through him. He moved his shaft into her one last time, plunging all of himself inside of her. She cried out. It took him a moment to realize that he had spent his seed and was resting his forehead against Alika's damp one. He heard her panting and realized he was breathing heavily as well. When he looked up, she flashed him an innocent, but satisfied smile.

"Did I hurt you?"

She shook her head and ran the tips of her fingers over his muscled chest. "Not at all. But I don't think you're completely satisfied. You're still hard inside of me." She wiggled, and he realized it was true. Their coupling had been exhilarating, but he needed more. It was a driving need, probably the excitement of the situation they were in.

He flashed her a smile and watched as Phillip's ass stuck up in the air as he pleasured Elarna. It fascinated him as he lifted Alika off him and strolled over to Phillip. He ran his fingers down the other male's spine, amazed at the contrast of his hand on such white flesh. Once he touched the supple skin, a spark of energy went through him. Alika trailed her fingers along Phillip's shoulder before leaning over and drawing Elarna's nipple into her mouth and sucking on it. Elarna thrusted her hips up at the touch and uttered something he couldn't understand. But seeing all of them gratifing one another drove him onward. It was too much to keep his hairless form. He threw back his head and roared, letting his normal form take over. As he grew and hair sprouted on his body, he heard Elarna cry out. She opened her eyes and there was a satisfied smile on her face. Herman rolled his shoulders feeling at home in his beastial shape and slipped his hand around Phillip's waist and grabbed his cock.

He worked Phillip's dick, running his hand up and down and saw the human male shiver as he manipulated him. Phillip glanced back at him and the hunger in the Earthling's eyes swept over him. Herman could feel Phillip's anticipation and his longing. Underneath all of that, there was another presence as feral as his own beast. As he worked him, Phillip's form began to change. It only took a moment as the seamless transition went from hairless to beast. His prick elongated in Herman's hands, and he found it made him harder. He wanted to continue and feel the Earthling come as his animal form, but Phillip growled something and pulled away from him. Herman tried to answer him, but before he could, he found himself shoved down onto the bed and Phillip was on top of him. The brown fur of the Bigfoot was dark against his own white fur.

"Mine," Phillip grunted and pushed himself along Herman's body. Their shafts touched. Hot and throbbing and yet sensitive all at the same time.

Phillip shut his eyes and grimaced as he rode Herman. The friction between them made Herman desire for release. The bed depressed around him. When he rolled over he saw a large, black feline on the other side of him, holding down his right arm. Staring into those eyes, he knew it was Elarna and saw how beautiful she was in her feline form. Another large animal that he understood to be Alika in a pelt of fur was weighing down his other arm.

The Bigfoot slid against him. Herman could barely hold on to the pleasure that coursed through him. He was going to give in to the yearning and the delight that coursed through all of them. They were all connected in some way. Sharing the same bed. He threw back his head and howled when Phillip bit into his shoulder. He thrust his hips forward and felt his release as well as the shudder of the male on top of him. His heart beat erratically and yet he was complete in a way he never had been before. Being with them was the right thing. He knew it in his heart.

The females released his arms and Phillip rolled off him until he was nestled between Alika and Herman. It took him a second to catch his breath, but when he did he turned and saw Elarna, his woman, was looking back at him with her normal face. He trailed his fingers along her jaw. She kissed the inside of his palm.

"Are you happy?" she asked.

"Yes," he said, glad the ship's translators were able to form his language into words she could understand while he was in this form. "Are you? With this?"

"Very. More than I ever thought I could be. Seeing you together with Alika and Phillip drove me wild."

"It seemed Phillip was making you very content. You enjoyed his mouth on you and his tongue?"

She nodded. "I did. And there are many more things I can show you. But just remember, you are the one I want to be with. No matter what happens on Rovan. You are my mate."

"And you are mine." He pressed his muzzle to her lips and kissed her gently.

Herman lay wrapped in the arms of the woman he loved and the two other aliens he had come to respect and think of as his friends. Sharing this intimate moment had cemented something between them. Elarna had shown him that his existence was not a curse. It was a gift.

He had learned that there was more out in the universe than he ever thought possible, and he was going to discover it with the woman he loved and his new found family.

The End

About the Author

Crymsyn Hart is a National Bestselling author of erotic romance and horror. Her worlds are filled with luscious vampires, gorgeous gods, quirky witches, and everything else that goes bump in the night. Crymsyn worked as a psychic for many years in Boston while attending Emerson College. She graduated with a BFA in Writing, Literature, & Publishing. Crymsyn shares her life with a small zoo, three playful puppies, and her hubby Mark.

Visit her on the web at:
www.RavynHart.com

PURPLE SWORD PUBLICATIONS
Romance and Speculative Fiction
www.purplesword.com

www.ingramcontent.com/pod-product-compliance
Lightning Source LLC
Chambersburg PA
CBHW072055170626
46813CB00004B/1359